Midlife Love Story
A Later in Life Grumpy Romance

PIPER SULLIVAN

Copyright © 2022 by Piper Sullivan

All rights reserved.

No part of this book may be reproduced in any form or by any electronic or mechanical means, including information storage and retrieval systems, without written permission from the author, except for the use of brief quotations in a book review.

Sign up to my Exclusive Romance Connoisseurs' Club to receive my Free Romance, Her Fake Fiancé Billionaire Boss.

CHAPTER 1
CARLOTTA

"You're here, thank goodness!" Pippa wrapped her arms around me, her ready-to-pop-any-day-now belly looming large between us as she tugged me and my bags inside the house. She pulled back with a sheepish smile and a small blush. "Sorry, I'm a little restless."

I laughed and shook my head. "That's an understatement. How are you feeling?"

Pippa shrugged. "I'm uncomfortable all the time, hungry just as much, and I miss Ryan." Her shoulders fell in disappointment, and she motioned for me to follow her into the spacious living room. "What're in the bags?"

"Dinner." I set the heavy-duty paper bags with the Dark Horse logo on the large square coffee table. "All put together by Nina, who misses the heck out of you." The chef at the restaurant Pippa managed was a genius in the kitchen, and I couldn't wait to see what she prepared for this impromptu girls' night to keep Pippa sane until the baby came. Or until Ryan returned to Carson Creek. Whichever came first.

Pippa tried to get on her knees to help unpack the bags, but there wasn't enough room between the sofa and the table for her and her belly. "Dammit," she sighed. "I'm so fat right now I can't even pig out properly."

"Not fat, pregnant," I clarified in my haughtiest southern belle tone. "I'll lay out the food Pippa, you go get some dishes and silverware for us. And glasses."

Pippa pouted and tried—and failed—to push herself from her purgatory spot wedged between the furniture. "This baby better be so darn cute that I forget that I can't even stand up without help."

I laughed and stood to help her. "Welcome to my world, only there's no cute baby I can blame."

Pippa scoffed. "Oh please, Carlotta, everyone in town admires your sexy curves, and the expert way you highlight them. You're practically the same size as when we were in high school." Pippa grabbed her boobs and then let them go dramatically. "When this baby comes, my boobs will be gone forever, along with all the other good bits that you have all the time."

I rolled my eyes at her compliment, I knew what I looked like. I was cute, some might even call my pretty, but my whole life my beauty queen mama told me that my curves were a problem for respectable clothes and careers. My body, she often said, was meant for making babies and nothing else.

"Whatever you say Pip," I told her and helped her up.

"Of course it's whatever I say. It's my house, and I'm fifty-two months pregnant, I dare you to argue with *that*."

I laughed and when I heard her shuffling around the kitchen, I turned my attention to unpacking dinner and thinking about Pippa and Ryan's baby. Their's was a romance novel worthy story of second chances and an unexpected pregnancy, and then, finally, reconciliation. They were lucky.

The doorbell rang, pulling me out of my envious thoughts and back to the present. "I got it," I yelled and went to open the door for Lacey. "Well aren't you a sun-kissed sight for sore eyes?"

Lacey's face flamed pink in a blush that made me laugh. "Thank you Carlotta. You look as good as you always do."

I rolled my eyes at the compliment. "Come on in, world traveler, you're just in time for dinner."

"Dinner?" Lacey's eyes went wide. "Was I supposed to bring something? Pip just said to come over and keep her company. I only brought booze, one non-alcoholic bottle for the mommy-to-be."

"Nah, she's always hungry, so I figured you can't have a girls' night without goodies." I shrugged as we made our way to the living room. "Oh, and Pippa is restless," I warned about two seconds before she put down the dishes and flung herself at Lacey.

"Wow, look at that tan! I guess Paris was as good as everyone says." She nearly hugged the life out of Lacey, who looked to me for an explanation, but all I offered was a shrug and a smile.

"Paris was amazing," she said on a long drawn out sigh. "We saw all the tourist traps, but with a guided tour, there was so much history to the city. And the last few days we got caught up in a protest, which turned into work for both of us." Her face glowed with happiness and satisfaction, something she'd worked hard to achieve. "It was incredible."

"That's so wonderful," Pippa shot back with a beaming smile, one hand absently stroking her round belly.

"I'm so happy for both of y'all," I told my friends sincerely. I truly was happy they'd both found love in their forties—again, or for the first time—but I couldn't help but wonder if that was in the cards for me. Maybe Mama and Daddy were right, and I shouldn't have turned my nose up at all those wealthy suitors from *good families* when I was younger. But back then I was determined to stand on my own, designer heeled feet.

It'll happen or it won't, something I told myself so

much over the past year that it was becoming my mantra. One I didn't want to think about now, if ever. "So Pippa, serious question?"

"Uh oh," she said, her eyes wide as she backed away from me and took her spot on the sofa where she promptly began plating up some of the food. "What did I do now?"

"Nothing," I laughed. "Just curious if you ever plan on marrying Ryan."

She huffed out an annoyed breath. "Technically, we're already married, we just haven't had a wedding. Yet."

Lacey scoffed. "You know good and well that if you don't have a big wedding, you're not really married. Unless you're planning on moving back to Chicago?"

"No," she answered quickly. "Not that. I do plan on having a wedding, a big white one. I gave in to a quick marriage with a Justice of the Peace because Ryan wouldn't shut up about being married well before the baby came, in case they ended up being good at math." She gave an affectionate eye roll. "I'm not giving up on being as hot as humanly possible at my wedding."

"Still not an answer," Lacey teased.

Pippa sighed and sank deeper into the sofa as she chewed her food. "As soon as this baby comes into the world safe and sound, we can start planning the wedding, and not a moment sooner."

I blinked at her tentative schedule. "You don't want to take a month or so to recover from childbirth?"

"Nah," she shook her head. "I have the rest of my life for that. I want a big wedding with a big white poofy dress. Elegant and upscale, but in a barn, and with lace and shimmery silver and gold everywhere. Oh and hay on the floor." She smiled and it lit up her entire face. She was overflowing with that in-love-and-happy-with-my-life glow that made me as jealous as I was thrilled for her.

But I couldn't help getting excited as her wedding theme started to coalesce in my mind. "Oh, and a second chance theme," I piped in. "You know like twice baked potatoes, fried chicken in one course and then chicken fried steak in another. You know, making things better the second time around?"

"Oh my god, I love it!" Pippa squirmed excitedly in her seat. "Like a miniature menu, but extended for the sake of elegance?"

"You're the bride-to-be," I assured her with a smile and turned to my meal. Everything was delicious, southwestern eggrolls, stuffed mashed potatoes, risotto balls and butter poached asparagus. "Damn this is so good I might have to make use of that gym membership I'm still paying for."

"Why?" Lacey shuddered visibly. "If I had those curves I wouldn't add one ounce of muscle to them."

I laughed. "I'm trying to avoid gaining ounces that quickly turn into pounds."

"Carlotta, Pippa and I have talked about ourselves nonstop, we didn't even think to ask about you. Horrible friends," she sighed, tears forming in her eyes.

"Don't worry about it. There's a reason I've been so quiet. Because I have no life outside of work and you girls, and therefore, there is nothing to tell. Nothing at all."

Pippa sighed, but a moment later her face twisted in pain and a low growl escaped.

I pushed to the edge of my seat and set my plate down, worry turning to acid in my belly. "Pippa, are you all right?"

She nodded after exhaling forcefully. "I'm fine. I just think that I'm going into labor!" The last word came out on an agonized shriek. "Yep, definitely labor."

Lacey gasped and her hands started to shake. "Labor? Isn't it too soon for that?"

"Soon?" Pippa spluttered. "This baby is three days overdue Lacey, so no it's not too soon. It's well past due thank you very much." She started to breathe too fast and I stood, going to her side right away.

"Slow down your breathing Pippa. Easy and slow," I tell her deeply inhaling and then exhaling slowly. "Yes, just like that. Exactly like that." Her eyes were wide, filled with worry and so many other emotions I couldn't name them, all while focusing on her breathing.

"Carlotta, I'm scared."

"Don't be," I smiled and tried to ignore my own growing fear . "You'll be fine. Women have been doing this for millions of years, and you're tougher than most women I know. Just keep breathing, in and out, slowly. Deeply."

She did as I did, taking her time breathing slowly.

"Hey Lacey, can you grab the bag in the closet by the door and put it in my car?"

Lacey stood and nodded, moving a few steps before she froze. "Wait, I can't drive your big ass car."

I smiled. My pearl-white Escalade was a monster if you weren't used to driving her, but it was perfect for carting around things for events, and I loved her. "Well, seeing as my only experience with childbirth is television, I figured you'd sit in the backseat and keep Pippa on the right track."

"Oh. Right." She nodded absently and went to do as I asked.

Pippa laughed. "She can spend a week in a South American jungle, but childbirth makes her squeamish."

"I think it's a little different when you're the one giving birth," I told her and stood, holding my forearm out for her to use.

"Thanks," she groaned and doubled over in pain. "Damn, they really undersold the pain of the contractions."

I laughed and wrapped one of her arms around my

shoulder as we made our way to the door. "Just think about the cute as a button baby you'll get from all this pain."

She nodded, and after a minute or two of maneuvering her into the back of my Escalade, Pippa was settled in the back with Lacey beside her while I hauled ass towards the hospital.

My thoughts remained half on Pippa being in labor, while the other half of my brain thought of all the things that were of no use to me in this moment. Such as the fact that I was forty-two years old and alone. No, not alone, I was childless. It wasn't something I expected to regret so soon, but with each passing day, as my relationship options dwindled, that became less and less of a possibility for me.

I had time, logically I knew that. Forty-two wasn't exactly ancient, even if my gynecologist made it seem that way every year, but it was old enough that every birthday would decrease my chances just a little bit more. "I don't hear any breathing back there!" I shouted over the growls of pain.

I drove on autopilot, but we made it much quicker than the usual fifteen minute drive. I let the girls off at the automatic doors before I went in search of a parking spot that wasn't in Outer Space. Since Lacey had childbirth experience, I sat in the waiting room, and as the dutiful friend, I called Ryan and Chase because they would both want to know. I called GG because he was about to be a grandpa again. And I called Valona because she was Pippa's best friend.

With my tasks complete, I sat and waited.

And waited.

Before I got bored and pulled my trusty tablet from my bag to make notes for Pippa's wedding, and to refresh my memory on all the things I had to do this week.

Plenty of tasks to complete. But not a date, or a booty call, or any other intimate activities on the schedule.

Such was the life of a soon-to-be spinster.

CHAPTER 2
CHASE

I hated shopping. Whether it was shopping for groceries, which I had to do regularly, or to buy clothes, shoes or household items, I hated it. But buying gifts for people, especially my sister? I hated it with the fire of ten thousand suns. It was impossible to get gift-giving right, no matter how well you knew the person. They were obligated to pretend they loved the gift, no matter how clumsy or awful or unwanted it was, but no one was a good enough liar to really sell that fake happiness. It was unnecessarily stressful when cash or a gift card was perfectly acceptable.

Except when it came to babies, and new mothers. My older sister, Pippa, was upstairs in the maternity ward having a baby. The first baby in a new generation of the Carson family, and that was a special occasion. Momentous, even. I called our parents, who were off in

New Zealand learning to surf or something equally ridiculous, and they shouted with joy and promised to make it back to Carson Creek.

Eventually.

They didn't even stay on the line long enough for me to ask what kind of gift I should get my sister and new niece or nephew, from all of us. Damn them.

So here I stood, inside the hospital gift shop's maternity section, feeling absolutely useless. Less than useless. How I could run an entire town with almost no assistance, aside from my actual assistant, CJ, but I couldn't figure out how to brighten my sister's day after pushing a baby from her body, was beyond me.

I didn't even know if she was having a boy or a girl yet, because Pippa in her usual stubbornness had decided she wanted to be surprised, making it impossible to get this gift thing just right. The first thing my eyes landed on was a giant stuffed giraffe that stood close to four feet tall. I grabbed the giant stuffed animal and tucked it under my arm, the sound of a tinkling laugh behind me shifted my attention from the wall of gifts to a familiar face.

Carlotta.

She leaned against a small display of sunglasses and paperback novels, with an amused smile. "What?" Whenever she was around, I got the distinct feeling she was mocking me somehow, like she had some secret, inside joke that only she was in on.

She shook her head. "Oh, nothing. Just wondering if you couldn't find anything bigger?"

My lips twitched in amusement as I took in the sheer size of the damn thing, and then I frowned. "What's wrong with this?"

"Nothing at all." Her smile remained fixed in place, always sweet and polite, and just a little bit sexy, as she sauntered over to where I stood. "Want some help?"

My shoulders sank with relief. "Yes, please."

She smiled a little wider and rested one hand on my shoulder. "It's nothing to be ashamed of Mr. Mayor, shopping for babies is hard if you don't know what you're doing."

"And you do?" She was, last I heard, just as single and childless as I was.

"No," she answered with a sigh, the light in her eyes dimmed a little. "But I have some professional experience. People with money go all out for baby showers, and I've seen it all, so let me pass on some of my knowledge to you."

"I'm sorry," I began, because I sensed that I'd said something wrong.

Carlotta held up a hand with light pink nails, her deep brown eyes full of sadness and regret, and gave a dismissive wave. "It's all right. I know the truth." She turned back towards the wall of products and plucked a few things from different racks.

"What's all this?" I shook my head, baffled at all the

stuff she'd grabbed. "She already had a baby shower, didn't she?"

"Yes, but one thing I've learned is that new parents can never have too many onesies, baby wipes, bibs and spit pads." Carlotta dropped the items in the basket at my feet and smiled up at me.

It was a dazzling smile, one that always made me feel as if I had her full attention, even as a boy. It was a special gift that served her well in her line of work, but it was hard to remember that when you were the focus of her attention. And she smelled so good too, floral, earthy and feminine. It was exactly how a woman should smell. Realizing I was just staring at her like a dopey teen, I cleared my throat and frowned at the shopping basket. "What the hell is a spit pad? And a onesie?"

Carlotta laughed, revealing the creamy curve of her neck and the swell of her breasts as she tilted her head back. "A spit pad is a cloth that will protect your suits from puke when you're burping your little bundle after a feeding. And onesies are like baby yoga pants, perfect for every occasion." She plucked several packages from the wall, in a variety of colors, none of which were pink or blue.

"Has the baby come yet?"

She nodded, her chocolate waves brushing against her shoulders. "Yep. You have, what I assume, is a very beautiful niece. I came down for some fresh air while the doctors got Pippa cleaned up and found you looking lost."

"A girl." I had a niece. A little girl who would need to be protected while her rock star father was on the road, entertaining the masses. "What are you doing with all these colors, then?"

Carlotta laughed again. "Your sister will go way over the top in perfectly pink girly stuff, and it's your job, as her favorite uncle, to make sure she has options. Like other colors, and stripes and polka dots."

"But...pink," I said weakly.

"It's your prerogative as Pippa's younger brother to annoy her, Mr. Mayor, use it."

I smiled. "I never realized you had a wicked streak Carlotta."

"Me?" She put a hand to her chest, tone perfectly innocent. "Why, thank you."

I rolled my eyes at her playful tone, but I couldn't help smiling. "My pleasure," I muttered and reached for a giant gift bag, and waited beside Carlotta while the cashier packed it all up for me.

"Here you are Mayor Carson. And congratulations on becoming an uncle."

"Thank you, Lisa. I hope I can be the uncle she needs." I turned to Carlotta and frowned. "You came with gifts?"

"No, this is Pippa's pregnancy bag. I'm taking it up to

her so she can get comfortable now that the hard part is over."

"You think of everything."

She laughed as we walked towards the elevator. "It's my job to organize and plan. It's what I do."

It was more than that, and her humility surprised me, but I didn't tell her that. Instead, I enjoyed the comfortable silence as the elevator carried us up to the maternity ward, the waiting room filled with pastel colors reminiscent of Easter. It was meant to be soothing, but I felt anything but soothed or calm.

"Where is everyone?"

"GG is probably on his way, same for Valona. The Gregory Brothers are out of town shooting a video or some other Hollywood thing." Her smile was soft and sweet, and full of sympathy for some reason. "You're not afraid to be alone with an itty bitty baby are you?"

I gritted my teeth before I could get my emotions in check. "No. Of course not. I'm just a little nervous."

She sucked in a shocked breath. "But you're so good with people. A little bit gruff, but good."

"At least I've got you fooled," I told her with a smile. "Babies are so tiny, and so easy to inadvertently hurt. They make me nervous."

"Or, they're so tiny and cute, and they smell so good. Think of it that way, and your nerves will fly, fly, fly away." Carlotta stepped away from the elevator and turned over her shoulder with a grin. "You coming?"

"Yes." My answer came out on a reluctant sigh, and I shook my head. "I'm not nervous to meet my niece, just to hold her."

Her smile spread slowly and her laugh was low and husky, supremely feminine. "Of course."

I stopped halfway down the hall when I realized I was alone with my oversized giraffe and bag of gifts. "You're not coming?"

Carlotta shook her head. "Nope. I think this moment is just for you and Pippa, just a family affair."

I nodded, even though I didn't really think it was necessary for her to stay behind. Carlotta was practically family, she'd been around forever, had grown up in Carson Creek. Over the past few years we'd spent many holidays together at the soup kitchen on Christmas, and the food pantry for Easter and Thanksgiving. If she wasn't family, what in the hell was she?

I shook off those thoughts as I stood in front of Pippa's room, nervous, because my sister was now a mother, and my niece was inside with her. After a quick pep talk, I gave the door a quick tap with my knuckles and went inside.

"I heard there was a special delivery in here?"

"Chase!" Pippa's blue eyes went wide with excitement. "You're here."

"Where else would I be?" I grinned. "I'm here to meet the newest addition to the family. Where is the little stinker?"

"Stinker? I'll have you know that my beautiful little girl smells like the softest, sweetest rose petal." She stuck her nose in the air and gave me her snootiest look. "Ryanna Mirabel Carson-Gregory. It's a mouthful I know," she rolled her eyes. "But my princess needs a big name to fit her big personality."

"So what you're saying is, that I'm getting another difficult female in the family?" She nodded primly. "I guess normal was too much to hope for."

"Better luck next time?'

"Yeah, I guess." I shoved my arms out clumsily. "These are for you. Well technically they're for Ryanna, but she's too young to appreciate them right now."

Pippa laughed again and held out her arms to receive her gifts. "Good thing for you that both me and Ryanna love gifts. Gimme."

"Greedy," I grumbled and handed over the giraffe first, and then the gift bag. "I hope you both like them."

"I'm pretty sure this sucker will serve as a jungle gym until she starts walking." She laughed and wrapped the giraffe in a big hug. "Thank you, Chase."

I spotted the little bundle wrapped up in pink in the little bassinette on the other side of the bed and hesitantly walked over. I thought she was sleeping at first, but her big hazel eyes were wide open and she sported a head full of wispy red curls. Her rosebud lips curved into a smile, but maybe that was just my imagination.

"She's so beautiful, Pip."

"Right?" She sighed and shook her head. "She is absolutely perfect Chase."

I couldn't argue with that, and when I reached down to touch her hand, her tiny chubby little fingers curled around my index finger. "Think I can hold her?" It was probably a stupid question, the baby was less than an hour old, and probably didn't need to be manhandled for a few days, but as I gazed down at her, I had a craving to just cuddle her.

"Absolutely. Just bend with your knees, and scoop her up like a football in the crook of your arm."

I did exactly as Pippa instructed, and I couldn't take my eyes off the tiniest bundle I'd ever held. "She's so small. So soft." Carlotta was right, babies do smell good. Really good. "Is she wearing talcum powder?"

Pippa laughed. "Baby powder, that's why you can't stop smelling her head."

I froze at her words, and pressed a kiss to Ryanna's forehead. "I wasn't smelling her, I was making sure I didn't kiss her soft spot."

"There is no soft spot."

It was my turn to laugh at my sister. "All babies have one, including this one."

She smiled softly, but I knew that look in her eyes, it was her mischievous look, and I knew I had to brace myself for whatever came next.

"So Chase, I have a favor to ask."

"And you waited until I had Ryanna in my arms so I couldn't run away?"

"Maybe?" She laughed and reached up to rub Ryanna's soft hair. "It's nothing big, just a teeny, tiny little favor."

I kept my gaze focused on Ryanna. She was tiny and beautiful, and so soft. "I'm listening."

"I need your help Chase."

"With?"

She sighed. "Planning the wedding." Pippa held up her hands before I could spit out the "no" that was on the tip of my tongue. "Carlotta is the official wedding planner, but she'll need some input, and since I'll be busy with Ryanna, I figured you could help with the details?"

"Anything but that Pip. Please." As a small town mayor, I attended more than my fair share of weddings, more than any single man would ever agree to, in fact. But this was my sister, and I couldn't let her down.

"All you need to do is help with the details so Carlotta can plan it all."

"What kind of details?" As Ryanna squirmed in my arms, I understood the appeal of babies. She was the perfect distraction, calming, so that I couldn't just freak out and shout at my sister for her outrageous request.

"Cake flavors. Invitation fonts, styles and colors, things like that."

I frowned. "That doesn't make any sense. You can

answer those questions on the phone or by email, and Carlotta knows you well, she knows all this stuff already." Something was going on, I was sure of it.

"She does, but this is different. This is *my* wedding, and I love Carlotta, a lot, and I'd love to not be another bridezilla she has to deal with. So can you help me? Pretty please?"

"Fine. I'll help. But only when my schedule allows it, Pip. This isn't going to become my full time job."

"I already told you, Carlotta is in charge."

I rolled my eyes at the smirk on her face. "Don't push it, I already told you that I'll do it." Then a wicked thought popped into my head, and I looked away from Ryanna with a grin. "Does this wedding planning count as my wedding gift?"

Pippa laughed, the sound startled Ryanna momentarily, but the little girl was moments from falling asleep in my arms. "I'll tell you what Chase, this planning can count as my wedding gift from you, *if* you bring a date to the wedding."

"Evil, evil woman."

She laughed again in response.

CHAPTER 3
CARLOTTA

Another wedding over and done with. I stood in the back of the reception hall that was part of The Old Country House estate wearing a satisfied smile as the happy couple enjoyed their first toast, immediately followed by their first dance. The groom looked at his bride as if she was his everything, as if she was the most beautiful woman—the only woman—in the whole entire world.

It was enough to give a woman like me hope that all wasn't completely hopeless. Valona and Pippa, even Lacey had all found love again later in life, and there really was no reason I couldn't do the same. Except I didn't think I could. Or would.

So I turned my focus back to where it had been for the past twenty-odd years, work. Event planning was something at which I excelled, taking a few details and turning it into a memorable event people would always think of fondly. Years of helping Mama throw parties for the important bigwigs in Carson Creek, down in Nashville, and all the surrounding, and more importantly, moneyed, parts of the city had finally paid off. My job was exhausting on the best of days, but events like this where everything flowed as it was meant to without any outrageous disasters made it all worth it.

Brides were meant to be out of control, given how much importance was placed on the wedding day for the woman. Everything had to be just perfect, picturesque and executed according to her twelve-year-old dreams, or it was a failure. I expected it from brides, and since brides helped me start my business, I gave them a lot of rope to hang themselves. But the non-wedding events? They had taught me a very valuable lesson, everyone had an inner-bridezilla.

But Jess and Mark were an adorable young couple from wealthy Knoxville families. They were easy to please, and Jess knew exactly what she wanted, which made my job incredibly easy. She'd fallen in love with The Old Country House and had insisted that Nina take care of all the food, agreeing to pay the Dark Horse fee even though the reception was elsewhere. They were dream clients, and I just knew it was to make up for the fact that my next event, a retirement party for a seventy-two year old vineyard owner, was going to be a nightmare.

Don't think about it, I told myself as Mark dipped Jess low over his arm and brushed the softest, sweetest kiss to her lips.

I couldn't change the next event. I'd accepted it, drawn up the contracts which had been signed. And the deposit had been paid. There was no backing out, even if I was the sort of planner who would back out. Which I most certainly was not.

"Enjoying yourself?" Chase's deep voice was much less gruff than it usually was, the low timber caused unexpected shivers to crawl up my spine.

I turned to face him and I had to stifle a gasp at how handsome he looked in his suit. Chase had an unorthodox look, with thick red hair that would curl immediately if he didn't keep it cut as short as he did, and bright green eyes the color of shamrocks. You couldn't tell normally that he de-stressed by boxing, but in the three-piece green and gold windowpane suit he wore, his wide chest and thick biceps were perfectly on display. My mouth went dry, and I had to swallow around the lump in my throat. "I always enjoy a good wedding, Mr. Mayor. You're looking very sophisticated today, in a professor-ly kind of way."

He laughed, but his pale, slightly freckled skin couldn't hide the blush that stained his cheeks. "Professor-ly?"

I nodded. "Yep. The windowpane print really suits you."

Chase rolled his eyes and I laughed. "What?"

"It's a compliment, the only acceptable response is *thank you Carlotta*."

His lips twitched in amusement. "Thank you, Carlotta," he replied formally.

"You are most welcome Mr. Mayor. Now tell me, how do you know the happy couple?" Chase often made an appearance at weddings or events involving the citizens of Carson Creek, but Jess and Mark were from Nashville.

Chase shrugged. "They want to do a test run of their new food truck venture here in Carson Creek, to see if the business plan has legs. We've been chatting."

"Food truck? That's a bit cosmopolitan for Carson Creek, but I think it could do well in a town like this."

His brows furrowed. "You do?"

"Sure, why not? Tourism in town is growing, and the population is getting younger. Besides, who doesn't love to grab a good taco by just rolling up to the curb?"

Chase's lips twitched with unspent laughter. "You don't strike me as a side-of-the-road-taco kind of girl, Carlotta."

I shrugged off the words, but I knew exactly how people saw me. I was the proper southern girl, a little bit stuck up, and girly as all get out. But that was my upbringing and my fashion sense. "I've got layers, Mr. Mayor, or haven't you heard?"

"I don't listen to rumors, only facts."

"In that case, the first tacos that roll off the truck are on me." I notched my chin a little higher and smiled.

Before Chase could utter another word, Margot was there in front of me with a nervous expression. "Sorry to interrupt Chase, but I really need to speak to Carlotta privately."

"Absolutely," he said in that always gruff tone. "Nice to see you Carlotta." His gaze lingered for a moment before he turned and walked away.

I gave Margot my full attention. "What's up?"

"I heard you were starting the plans for Pippa and Ryan's wedding. Do we have a date? Anything confirmed?"

"No," I sighed. Margot had made The Old Country House happen. It was her dream, her baby, and her land. But she was a Type A to the extreme, which could be a lot to deal with at times. "This week I'll put the wedding book together and send you whatever tentative dates I have."

"Okay great," she sighed and her shoulders sagged in relief. "It would be embarrassing if the town's biggest star didn't get married at our premier event space."

"Incredibly," I agreed, my tone mock-serious.

"Carlotta," she sighed. "I'm allowed to stress about this."

"You absolutely are, stress away," I assured her. "But you are not allowed to stress me out about it, not when

I'm juggling multiple events per week, and most of them are held on this estate."

"All right." Margot nodded absently, her violet eyes bounced around the room as they took in every detail. "This is gorgeous Carlotta. Would you mind if I took a few photos to use as inspiration?"

"Not at all." Before I could tell her to stay out of the photographer's way, Margot had her sleek, rose gold phone in hand, snapping photos of everything from the table settings and centerpieces, to the layout and glassware. "All right." With another problem solved, sort of, I went to check on the cake.

After the cake was cut, I could relax until it was time to round up all the single folks to catch the bouquet and the garter.

Weddings, am I right?

CHAPTER 4
CHASE

I sat in my office behind the cumbersome oak desk that was supposed to be a piece of Carson Creek history, but really it was just a massive piece of furniture that took up more space than it needed to. I'd tried to change it several times, but the uproar within city hall was so loud that at the end of the day, it wasn't worth the headache. At least not for me, when my schedule was always filled with tasks to complete, activities to attend, and most dreaded of all, documents to sign.

I loved being able to improve the lives of the people in my hometown, but getting to that point was a gigantic headache most days. Like today. Paperwork was strewn across half of my desk, all of it needed my signature, but I needed to be certain of what I was signing, so I constantly referred to my laptop for details. Back and forth between the two sides of the desk, it was a wonder I didn't spend most of the day dizzy.

"Yeah," I growled at the soft knock on my door, assuming it was my assistant CJ. "What is it?"

I didn't bother to look up when the door opened, because CJ knew to only interrupt me when it was important, and she hadn't said anything yet, so I assumed it was coffee or more documents to sign. The silence went on, and then the familiar scent of roses tickled my senses. Expensive roses. I knew that smell, and I remembered it well. When I looked up, there she was.

"Carlotta. Hi."

Her plump lips pulled into a grin. "Mr. Mayor. Is this a good time or should I come back when you're not quite so grumpy?"

It was hard to get mad when she was smiling at me like that, so I shook my head and waved her in. "Come on in. And I'm not grumpy."

Her melodic laugh bounced off the walls. "If that's your not-grumpy voice, I think we're all in trouble."

Pippa always called me grumpy, but I really wasn't, my voice just sounded like that. Some people have resting bitch face, and I have resting grumpy voice. "This is a nice surprise. What brings you by?"

Her brows arched in suspicion. "It's a nice surprise?"

My face morphed into a scowl. "Yes. Why wouldn't it be?"

Carlotta shrugged, the move drew my attention to her almost bare shoulders. She had on one of those sexy, feminine dresses that hugged her top half and flared out at the bottom, showing off her legs and a pair of heels that looked more like torture devices. But hot torture devices.

"I don't know, it always seems as if you're annoyed with me for some reason." She shrugged again, this time as if that didn't really bother her.

"I can assure you that is not the case." To prove my point, I waved her in to have a seat. "Dammit," I growled and stood, rushing around the desk to remove the stacks of folders and books taking up the seat I'd just offered to her.

She looked around the cluttered office with a blank expression. "Are you getting ready to move offices?"

"I wish," I grumbled. "I need more shelving in here, but I don't want to forfeit my workspace or my peace and quiet for a full week just to get them done." CJ had said the contractor would take a week to complete the project, so I put it off again, and again.

Carlotta said nothing for a long moment as she looked around my cluttered office, nodding as if taking notes inside her head. "Okay. Hang on." She held a finger up and pulled out her phone, thumb swiping quickly while she ignored me. I opened my mouth to growl at her for stopping by uninvited only to make a phone call, but her next words stopped me.

"Hey Grady, it's Carlotta." She laughed and tilted her head back, almost in a flirty way.

Grady? The bartender? Were they seeing each other?

"I'm good, thanks for asking. How are you?" She listened with a smile as the bearded bartender said whatever he said. "That's good to hear. If you want to throw an event to advertise it, I'll give you the friend's discount." She laughed again and my nostrils flared. "Right. Does your barback still do construction and carpentry? Because I need a small job done for a big client, and it's gotta be done over one weekend." She set her red purse down and pulled out a small, flowered notepad and pen to jot down some things in a quick scribble. "Perfect. Thank you, I'll call right now."

She turned to smile at me before she went right back to her phone and dialed another number. "Jameson? It's Carlotta."

"Another call?"

She turned to me and pointed to the phone. "Yep, that's me, the lady with the dresses." She laughed and rolled her eyes, before asking a few questions about something I didn't pay attention to, because her lush red lips moved nonstop, and I couldn't look away. "You can? That's great! I'll give Mayor Carson your phone number so you guys can talk details. Thanks again Jameson." Whatever he said made her blush. "I'll keep that in mind. See you soon." Carlotta ended the call and dropped the phone back into her bright red purse as she turned to me with satisfied grin. "Ask and you shall receive."

I blinked. "But I didn't ask for anything." Had I?

"Didn't you?" Her gaze swept the room again. "I guess I must have heard what you were thinking, then."

"Um, thanks for whatever that was."

She laughed and walked over to me, removing the stack of books and papers from my hand and setting them on the floor beside the chair. "That was a friend doing a favor for a friend. We're friends aren't we Chase?"

I'd known her my entire life, but we hadn't exactly been friends because of the age difference. As kids it seemed so vast, but lately it didn't seem to matter as much. "I would say acquaintances, but those are a type of friends, so sure, we're friends."

"I appreciate your honesty Mr. Mayor."

She did? Most people didn't appreciate my honesty, or what they deemed my constant briskness. "Thank you. I think."

Her big brown eyes stared at me and for the first time I noticed they were shaped like almonds, giving her a slightly exotic appearance. Had Carlotta always been so pretty? I wasn't sure about before, but I'd noticed a lot over the past week. "We have a few matters to discuss."

"We do?"

She nodded and reached inside what I now knew must be a clown purse, because the giant binder she pulled out from said purse couldn't have possibly been in there. "Yes, we have a wedding to plan."

I groaned and dropped my forehead to my desk. "I thought, or maybe I hoped that Pippa had forgotten. New mom brain or something."

"Sorry, but she didn't forget. In fact, Pippa called me to let me know you were my planning buddy in her place, just to make sure you didn't wiggle out of it." She dropped the thick binder on my desk with a thud. "I assure you that I won't forget either."

Carlotta was a force of nature, and I knew that first hand when she last marched up to my office to tell me that she was planning my election night party, and then months later, my inauguration party. She didn't ask, she told me, insisted it would be perfect. And it was.

So today I watched her lips pull into a slow, satisfied grin as I gave my reluctant acceptance of what was to come. "What do I need to do?"

She relaxed into the chair and crossed her legs. "Input mostly," she said with a sympathetic smile. "I have some clue about what Pippa wants, but when it comes to things like favorite cake flavors, colors, themes and things like that, I'll be counting on you."

Yeah, okay. "Pippa lives here in town, so why do I have to do this?"

"Because," she sighed with infinite patience. "Pippa has a brand new baby, which means she probably won't get much sleep and when she does, it won't be during regular hours. I'll do the heavy lifting, but when you stop by to see Ryanna, you can get her approval on things." Carlotta sucked in a deep breath, a move that made her ample cleavage swell. She let it out slowly. "I know it seems odd, but I don't have time to go back and forth while planning other events."

I nodded. Her explanation made perfect sense. Sort of. "How am I supposed to know what kind of cake she wants for her wedding?"

She shrugged. "For starters, she's your sister."

True. "And if you wanted to know what kind of cake she liked at sixteen, I could tell you. She hasn't lived in Carson Creek for years, and I'm just getting to know her again."

"Excellent." She nodded triumphantly. "You'll get to know her again, and pass what you learn to me so we can get this wedding planned."

"All right. I'm a man of my word, so we're in this together. Do you have a schedule?"

Carlotta shook her head, thick brown ringlets danced as she did. "I will have a schedule as soon as Pippa gives me a wedding date or a venue. In the meantime I brought lunch."

Now I was convinced that the red purse was magical, because she produced a brown bag with the Dark Horse logo on the front. "I appreciate the gesture, but we don't have anything to discuss."

"True," she nodded agreeably. "We can discuss you.

What do you do for fun? What do you like about being mayor?" As she asked the questions, she laid out a simple lunch of bison chili cheese fries, salad and sauteed mushrooms.

I blinked at her thoughtful questions. No one asked me what I liked about my job, most of them assumed it was the power or something equally tedious. "For fun, I read mostly. Though I have been known to binge watch documentaries."

She blinked in surprise. "History? True crime? What kind of documentaries?"

"Those are my favorites," I answered in surprise.

"Lucky guess. Me too. And being mayor?"

I shrugged because I felt uneasy answering the question, but Carlotta didn't seem to have an ulterior motive for asking. "I like knowing that the things I do here, bringing in new businesses, getting the streets re-paved, all of those little things help to make everyone's life a little better whether they know it or not." That sounded silly.

"I know what you mean. No one thinks of the ribbons tied to candles but without them, they would feel like something is missing. It's nothing like what you do, but I get it." She smiled and stood, smoothing her hands over her pretty little dress.

"You provide the details for the most important day of a couple's life, that's not nothing Carlotta."

"Maybe not," she said and offered me a quick smile

before she cleared the desk of our leftover lunch. "But the stop sign you had put in at the corner of Mint Street and North, probably saved a lot of injuries. Not to mention the speed bumps that are now on the school bus routes."

Her words floored me and filled me with warmth. The fact that anyone else had seen it that way felt special to me. "Thank you for saying that Carlotta."

She stood and flashed a grin. "Just telling the truth, or should I say facts?" She arched a brow and sent me one final grin before she left my office.

That was a strange encounter, and it was minutes after Carlotta was gone that I realized I hadn't asked her a thing about herself.

No wonder I'm still single.

CHAPTER 5
CARLOTTA

"Another mint julep please." I rapped my knuckles on the long wooden bar, and blew a stray strand of hair out of my face. This retirement party was determined to be the death of me, and weeks like this made me wish I had an assistant to delegate tasks to, because the wife of the retiree was driving me out of my dang mind.

Grady's big body created an intimidating shadow over me and I looked up at his thick red beard, bald head and big clear blue eyes. His arms were massive as they folded across his chest, brows arched in concern.

"Rough day?"

I nodded and finished the last sip of my cocktail. "The worst day and the longest week of my life, but I won't bore you with the details. Let's just say that it's a three mint julep kind of day, so please don't let me have more than that." Mrs. Rochester was determined to make this the most difficult retirement part in the history of the whole world. The woman had opinions and ideas on everything, no matter how far-fetched. How ridiculous.

Grady flashed that gorgeous smile of his that made all the female bar patrons lose their ability to think straight, and leaned forward on his impressively thick and corded tattooed forearms.

"You got it." He walked away to get my second drink, leaving me all alone with my thoughts.

It wasn't just Mrs. Rochester that had contributed to a long and stressful week. It was also my daddy. He'd called to set me up with some fancy pants lawyer from Biloxi, who would, in his words, take care of me. As if I needed some man to take care of me. If that was the case, I would have let them set me up with some rich, blue-blooded jerk ages ago. No, I needed a man who wanted me with all my curves, flaws and all, not someone who would try to change me to fit their social circle.

No way. Now how, and no thank you.

"Thank you Daddy, but I'm not interested in leaving Carson Creek, and especially not for a stranger."

His tone was annoyed, perturbed even, like I was some petulant child. "Carlotta you are far too old to still be single. It's not cute, it's verging on pathetic. Who will take care of you when you get bored of planning parties?"

I'd sucked in a breath at his words and his tone. "I don't need anyone to take care of me. I take care of me. My career more than pays the bills."

"It's not appropriate Carlotta. You're over forty and unmarried. People will start to wonder about your proclivities."

My proclivities, he'd said, and I'd rolled my eyes. "I don't give a damn what people think about my proclivities. Half of your friends are in loveless marriages, more than half if I'm being honest, and I'd rather be alone than stuck with a man I can't stand."

I knew my parents wanted the best for me, the only problem I have with that is that they want for me what they *think* is right for me, not what I actually want. They just want me to marry some wealthy man so they can stop worrying about me, it's not actually about me. Since I turned forty a few years back, Mama and Daddy had increased their pressure, and I had to push back even harder.

"You sure you don't wanna talk about it?" Grady stood in front of me with another mint julep in his big hands, worry in his blue eyes as he slid the drink my way.

I shook my head. "I'm sure, and I'm fine, thanks. Really, I am. Mostly I am just annoyed as hell, and I don't want to talk about it because it only increases my annoyance." I sighed and tried for a smile. "What's new with you Grady?" He was handsome, and his lush red beard only made my mind wander to another red head.

He let out an amused laughed, his gaze never wavered, not even when a group of hot twentysome-things strolled in, a cloud of giggles and cigarette smoke surrounding them. "Nothing. Got some new booze in, as you already know. I'm renovating my game room at my house, and that's about it." It was difficult to imagine a guy like Grady who owned a bar and had an arm full of tattoos owning a house.

I nodded. "Are you seeing anyone?"

"No," he growled, a deep, low, masculine sound. "You asking?"

I sighed and shook my head, wishing I had the guts to go after a guy like Grady, but the truth was he scared me. "Just making conversation. What do you do Grady, when you're not making drinks and dispensing advice?"

"Lots of outdoor activities. Hiking and skiing. Drinking and women." He grinned on the last two, as if they were obvious choices.

I smiled back. "Sounds exciting. I've skied once, but that's it, and it was an awful time. Is hiking fun? Have you ever tried rock climbing?" Grady's life actually sounded wonderful. He was under no obligations, no pressure from others to find a wife and have kids. "How old are you Grady?"

His lips twitched in amusement. "Thirty-one."

"Wow, that young?" I couldn't believe he was basically a baby. "Do your parents ever get on you about settling down?"

"All the time," he admitted with a sheepish grin. "I tell them the more they harp on me, the longer I'll stay single out of spite.

I laughed at his brilliant strategy. "Does that actually work?"

He nodded. "For a few weeks anyway."

I laughed again. "Maybe I should try that."

"You definitely should, it'll shut them right up. Unless of course, you have some trust fund that's dependent on you walking down the aisle and pushing out a baby before forty."

My smile brightened. "Well, well, look who's trying to get a bigger tip with the compliments. It's totally working, another mint julep, please." I mulled over Grady's advice while I sipped my cocktail, thinking about the state of my life. I was single, sure, but I also had a great career, a beautiful home and really good friends. My life was good. It was fine, more than fine, even. Would I love to find a good man to share my life with? Absolutely, but it wasn't a priority. I wanted the right man, not just any man. "To shutting up the naysayers," I offered a little louder than necessary as I raised my glass a few seconds too late.

Grady smirked at me as he reached under the bar and produced a bottle of water. "Fuck those naysayers," he added and crashed his plastic bottle against my glass.

"Exactly," I agreed and took another, slow sip. The icy liquid slid down my throat and the delicious mint flavor soothed my frazzled nerves. Some, anyway. "Hey Grady, would you be willing to rent this place out for events?" The bar was a little rough around the edges, but it had a certain charm that would be perfect for very specific events.

I sensed his hesitation before my gaze found his. "I never thought about it to be honest with you."

"Well I don't have anything lined up, but I'd love it if you thought about it. Figure out what you would like to make for an open bar, and for bar service, with or without bartenders provided by you or a catering service."

"No one works behind my bar but me."

I rolled my eyes. "Okay, then."

"You really think people would want to rent this place for events?" His surprise was evident, which was strange because he seemed to love this place.

"I do. Bachelor and bachelorette parties for one, retirement parties, divorce parties, all kinds of events that don't need to be so fancy. I think I could sell it, so you know, let me know."

He nodded and ambled down to the other side of the bar where a small group was waving money to get his attention. He worked hard and he didn't deserve that kind of attitude, but it didn't seem to bother him, so I calmly sipped my drink.

I played with the idea of having another mint julep, but I decided to just head home. Alone, as usual.

"Anything else, Carlotta?"

"Nah." I shook my head and pulled some cash from my wallet. "It's time to kick off these shoes and binge watch something until I fall sleep. Thanks for the delicious drinks, though. You're my favorite bartender Grady."

"Your *only* bartender," he growled back with a grin.

"You don't know everywhere I get my drinks, smarty pants." I left a good tip and walked home, happy that I didn't twist an ankle or worse after too much alcohol. "Home sweet home."

This was my place, my solitude, the place where I could be ugly and wear yoga pants while I ate too much popcorn.

Here I could just be me.

CHAPTER 6
CHASE

I spent at least ten minutes on Monday morning staring at the newly installed shelves in my office. Ten minutes was a lot, particularly for a man not given to effusive praise or even much in the way of noticing a woman's new hairstyle, shoes or even that a close friend had switched girlfriends. But on that Monday morning, I not only noticed the beautiful shelves that had been made to my exact specifications, including a lighter wood in preparation for my transition to a smaller, less historically significant desk.

"Wow."

Carlotta had come through in a big way, and I was determined to do the same for her when it came to planning my sister's wedding. I hadn't done much research on what it took to put on a wedding, or even the questions I needed to ask Pippa, but I would. If for no other reason than to return the huge favor she had done me by getting the shelves installed, and quickly.

A knock sounded on the door, but before I could answer, CJ strolled in with a bounce in her step. "Hey Boss, what's up?"

"Just admiring my new shelves. Aren't they great?"

CJ shrugged, her blue gaze narrowed at the still empty shelves. "They're all right, I guess."

"All right? They're beautiful, sturdy and most of all, done without interfering with my work." Carlotta really was a miracle worker and I needed to thank her. Personally.

"If you hadn't been so stubborn, Jess would have done a much better job than whoever did this." Her dismissive wave towards the shelves was unusually spiteful, and I stared at her for a long moment before I shook it off. CJ was young, and probably cared more that I hadn't used her contact than she let on.

"Well I'm satisfied, and the shelves are done. Now I can stack stuff and get some breathing room in here again." Without the clutter of books and notepads everywhere, I hoped to increase my daily productivity.

CJ turned slowly from the bookshelf, a smile on her face. "I can help."

I shook my head. "Thanks, but that's not necessary. If I put everything away, then I'll know where it is when I need it."

She twisted her red lips into a pout. "That's what

you have me for, to do insignificant things like this for you." There was something odd about her voice, something I couldn't quite name, and didn't bother trying.

"And you do plenty of that, but this I can do for myself." I had an assistant because if I had to answer every call and email that came my way, I'd never actually get any work done. "I think I'll do that first, while you catch up on the emails."

"You want coffee? Or maybe you're more in the mood for tea?"

"I'm good CJ, thanks." I gave my shelves one final look and returned to my desk, waiting for CJ to make her exit. When she was gone, I settled comfortably in my seat and picked up my phone, tapping a number that was becoming more familiar with each passing day.

The phone rang twice before a slightly husky, very melodic voice answered. "Hello, Mr. Mayor."

I chuckled and felt my body slowly relax under her playful tone. "You can call me Chase, you know Carlotta."

There it was again, that secret laugh of hers. "I know your name Chase, but being elected mayor is a big deal and you deserve to hear the title as much as you can. But," she drew the word out long its very own song, "if it makes you feel better, I'll call you Mayor Chase."

"If you really must." She laughed again and I felt my own smile brighten. "I called to tell you that the shelves are done, and they look fantastic. My office almost feels like a brand-new room, there's so much room on the floor, lots of free space."

"Does that mean you'll be doing your morning yoga sessions in your office now?"

"Yoga? Hardly." I preferred combat sports, something that made me sweat and get rid of some of the daily stress that had a tendency to build up if left unchecked. "I still can't believe you got this done so quickly. How?"

"The sheer force of my will," she said around another feminine laugh. "The truth is that craftspeople love to work, and my vendors love me because I reward good work with more work. I'm just happy that you're happy."

"I am beyond happy Carlotta, and I feel like *thank you* is an inadequate response." I could send her flowers or a basket, but that felt like something you'd do for an aunt who helped you land a job interview. "How about dinner?" The line fell silent for so long I wondered if she'd hung up to avoid the embarrassing rejection, or if I'd shocked her into unconsciousness.

"A meal as a way to say thank you?"

"Um, yeah," I swallowed nervously.

"How can I resist?" I could hear the smile in her voice and I smiled in return, wishing we were on a video call so I could see her face.

"You can't?" I wasn't sure if she meant the offer was too good to turn down, or that she couldn't say no because I'm the mayor and her wedding planning assistant.

"I rarely turn down a good meal, especially if it's free, and especially if the company is good. So you figure out all the details, do a little planning, to prepare yourself for your upcoming wedding planning."

I groaned at her reminder. Carlotta laughed again. "It won't be so bad, I promise. I'm very good at my job, Mayor Chase."

"I'm very good at my job too, but it doesn't happen to be wedding planning."

"You're good at details though, and that's mostly what I need from you, Chase. You'll see. I'm happy you like your new shelves, maybe I'll pop by one day soon to get a look at them myself."

The call ended before I could tell her to stop by anytime, and still I smiled. That woman was a whirlwind, but she was a fun whirlwind who spoke her mind.

Even though we were just friends, the more time I spent with Carlotta, the more I grew to like her.

CHAPTER 7
CARLOTTA

I was going to have dinner with a man.

Okay that man was Chase, mayor of Carson Creek. But he was still a man, and he was still taking me out to dinner, so it counted. Of course, that was probably because I hadn't been on an actual date in about a million years, so anything that was close to a date, or date-adjacent, I would accept with open arms.

It was just Chase, and I didn't mean that in a disparaging way, only that Chase and I were friends. Strictly friends. But I was also a friend who loved to get dressed up like every single day was a special occasion, it was one of the habits my mama taught me that stuck. I browsed my closet in search of something that wasn't too sexy, but not at all demure. Something that was eye-catching and would boost my confidence, but not so much that I gave Chase the wrong idea.

Eventually, with just thirty minutes to spare, I settled on a red slip dress that showed off my curves and hid the extra inches around my middle. I paired the outfit with my favorite black stilettos, they had gold heels, and I loved them to death. After I touched up my hair and makeup, I was ready to go. With just fifteen seconds to spare.

I took advantage of being ready early with a long, slow, studious perusal of my reflection, making sure not one hair was out of place and not one speck of lipstick stained my teeth.

I looked good.

I felt good.

But I also felt something else. Off. Nervous, even.

It was a strange sensation that I didn't want to think too hard about. Thankfully I didn't have to, because the doorbell rang at seven o'clock sharp, because this was Chase, and the man was as punctual as they came.

My black stilettos didn't fail me as I hurried down the stairs, stopping at the door for one last, long deep breath before I opened the door with what I hoped was a friendly smile.

"Chase, holy hotness! You look...good." Good was an understatement, but it wouldn't be right to pant over a nice man taking me out to dinner as a gesture of gratitude. "You look nice, Chase."

"Thanks," he answered nervously, unable to stop the

blush that crept up his neck and face. His hands moved nervously down his dark green blazer with the navy blue vest underneath, down to his dark jeans with a crisp crease down the center. He looked chic. And sexy. Two things I had never associated with Chase until this moment.

I need to get a real date if I'm lusting after the grumpy mayor.

"Come on in," I told him in a breathy voice I didn't recognize. "I just need to grab a sweater and my purse." I rushed upstairs and came back down in less than two minutes, breathless, anxious, excited and ready to go. "Ready?"

Chase turned and I saw the heat flare in his eyes when he took in my appearance. Those green eyes took a long, slow journey from head to toe and back to my face again. "You always look great Carlotta, you know that, but this is...wow."

"Wow? I'll take it, and cherish that compliment, Mayor Chase."

His lips quirked up into an amused grin and he held out his arm for me. "Shall we?"

"Sure. Yes. I mean, let's go." He flashed a wobbly smile that straightened when I took his arm.

"So, where are we off to for dinner?" I assumed we would show up at one of the restaurants in town and send tongues wagging for a few days.

Chase said nothing, only smiled as he helped me into his shiny black car, closed the door and jogged around to the driver's side door. "That is a surprise. Do you like surprises Carlotta?"

"I don't *not* like them, then again I can't remember the last time I was surprised by anyone. Well except for Lacey running off to cover unrest in Venezuela."

He laughed. "That was pretty unexpected." Chase handled the car well, driving slightly over the speed limit as we immersed ourselves in conversation.

"What about you, any urges to travel?"

"Maybe. Some day. I've always wanted to see the world, but when you decide to run for mayor, well you have to stay close to home."

"I guess I hadn't thought about that. Well you're near the end of your first term, which means in about five years you'll be free to roam the world with a scruffy face and sunburn."

He let out a gruff laugh. "Maybe the scruff, but I'll pass on the sunburn."

"Ah, the plight of the fair-skinned redhead."

"It's no joke," he shot back with a teasing smile. "Sometimes I get a bit burnt even on overcast days."

"You ought to look into being a guinea pig for SPF 1000 or something like that, I'm sure that's a thing."

"Believe me, I have the strongest sunblock you can legally buy, so don't think I won't try it if the option becomes available."

We drove on the interstate for about thirty minutes, chatting and falling into comfortable silence before we finally arrived at the restaurant.

"Barbecue?"

CHAPTER 8
CHASE

A big ball of worry formed in my gut and worked its way up to lodge in my throat. The look Carlotta sent me had stopped me cold, because upon further reflection, it probably wasn't the smartest idea in the world to take a classy woman like her to a barbecue themed restaurant.

"Yeah?" She was a southern girl through and through, and I figured she would appreciate the unique nature of this particular restaurant.

But there was an ear-splitting squeal followed quickly by a stunningly beautiful smile that made her brown eyes sparkle.

"Barbecue! Did you know that I absolutely love barbecue in all of its shapes, forms and varieties?" Her cheeks were flushed with excitement, and finally my shoulders dropped below my ears.

At her expectant look, I felt put on the spot and blinked several times. "No actually, I didn't know." At her wide-eyed expression, I shrugged. "They have all types of barbecue here though, Texas, Memphis, Carolina, Korean, Chinese, Japanese, Tandoori and even Brazilian." Feeling ridiculous, and like a waiter, I rolled my eyes. "Plenty more, but too many to name. I thought it would be a fun place to check out."

Carlotta grinned, her gaze full of happiness and excitement. "Well this is an absolutely wonderful surprise Chase. Thank you." She hooked her arm through mine and gave it a squeeze. "Lead the way Mayor Chase."

I groaned and she giggled as we made our way inside the restaurant and were quickly seated. A server appeared before we'd even looked at our menus. "What sounds good, Carlotta?"

She nibbled her lip as her eyes bounced over the drinks menu, but I knew the moment she spotted what she wanted, because her eyes flashed. "I'll have the spiked sweet tea, please."

"And I'll have the regular sweet tea."

"All right. Take your time with the menu, and I'll be right back with your drinks. The back pages have all the tasting menu items we have just in case you folks want the full global culinary experience." The server flashed a smile and jaunted off, leaving us alone.

All alone.

I expected some type of awkwardness to fall over me as we both focused on the menus in front of us, but there was none. It was an easy, comfortable silence while it lasted.

"What do you think, Chase? Are we going around the world together, or are we taking separate journeys?"

It almost felt like she was talking about more than the menu, but what that *more* could be, I didn't want to assume, so I shrugged and reminded myself this was just a dinner between friends. "That depends, Miss Carlotta, where would you like to go," I drawled.

"Mayor Chase has a goofy side. Who'd have thunk?" Carlotta leaned in, her chin resting in her hand as she examined me closely, a little too closely for my own comfort. "What other secrets are you hiding in there?"

I leaned in too, we were so close that I could see threads of gold and yellow in her eyes, and this close, they really did sparkle. "Tell me what you want to eat, and maybe I'll tell you."

Her eyes went wide in surprise and she sat back with a slow exhale. "I want one with all the Asian barbecue options."

My gaze dropped down to the menu and I scanned the list, finding the perfect one to fit her wants as well as mine. "How about the Slow Roll Around the World?"

Carlotta looked down for a long moment and then back up with a slow burn of a smile. "I'm game if you are."

When the server returned, I placed our order and turned back to this woman who I was now seeing in a whole new light.

"How's your family?"

She shook her head. "Oh no you don't, Mr. Mayor. You're giving up your secrets first."

I grinned again. "Nothing slips by you Carlotta. Maybe you should switch to politics."

"I don't think I'm diplomatic enough for politics, or as good at changing the topic as you are."

"Off the record?"

She laughed. "You're confusing me with Lacey, but sure Chase, your secrets are safe with me."

She'd called me by my name, not my title, or a combination of the two. "Fine, you want to know a secret? I do combat sports. Boxing and kickboxing, Muay Thai and Jiu jitsu." It wasn't something I bragged about, because for me it wasn't something to brag about, just something I did to stay fit and sane.

"Wow, so you're like, some kind of undercover badass."

"I like that you think so, but I'm not." I played football in high school, but I wasn't a star player or a bench rider, I was an all-right player. But in college and beyond, I'd won a few titles for my skills.

"Oh, don't be modest now that the secret is out. Do you travel for tournaments and stuff like that?" Her eyes were lit, and her interest made me want to share more with her.

"Yes. Not since becoming mayor, but I have a few ribbons and trophies."

"Wow, that's really exciting. And impressive."

"You think so?"

She nodded quickly. "Absolutely. I tell myself that getting my steps in each day is enough exercise for a woman my age, and here you are, working out for your health *and* for a competitive edge." Carlotta shook her head as if she was at a loss for words, which worked out perfectly as the first few dishes arrived.

I wasn't comfortable with the compliments, as much as I appreciated them. Her effusive words felt sincere, which only made me feel like a fraud. I wasn't some badass, some tough guy, quite the opposite. "Not for a competitive edge, just because it's something I enjoy, and I have earned the skills to qualify to compete."

"Are there spectators at these events?"

"There are. Not like football or basketball, but the turnout can be impressive for the bigger tournaments."

Her brows were knitted into a straight line. "Will you tell me the next time you have one? It sounds like something I have to see."

"Um, sure."

She flashed a quick smile and bit into the Brazilian barbecue. "Damn that's good." Her eyes closed, and she took another bite before they opened on me. "You have to try it." She held her hand up to my mouth, a juicy piece of meat between her thumb and forefinger. "Come on, try it."

Suddenly my zipper grew painfully tight, and I swallowed hard. What in the hell was going on with me? How could I be experiencing this physical reaction to Carlotta Montgomery, a woman I'd known since I was a kid? She'd always been beautiful with an abundance of curves, but I'd never reacted to her like this. After talking my body back from the edge, I smiled and opened my mouth. She slid the meat between my lips and pulled her hand back slowly, just as my tongue swept over her fingertips.

She gasped.

"That *is* spectacular."

Her brown eyes were still wide, her mouth slightly parted in something that looked a hell of a lot like attraction. Desire. "Told ya," she said, her voice slightly breathless.

Dinner was great, if a little agonizing with all of Carlotta's moaning and sensual eye rolls. Conversation flowed freely, better than any real dates I'd been on in the past year.

The server showed up a few minutes after we finished our last few bites. "Room for dessert? We have an excellent brownie pie, or if you'd like, a brisket brittle."

Carlotta groaned. "Please tell me that is as heavenly as it sounds."

"More than heavenly," the server said with a smile.

"I'll have an order of that, to go please."

"Make it two," I added just before we were left alone again. "Wicked woman."

"Thank you?" She laughed, and the sound filled me with genuine warmth. Heat too, but also the warmth of affection.

"My pleasure." I meant those words deeply. Carlotta was the friend I didn't know I needed. She was playful, and didn't let me take myself too seriously without diminishing my job as a small town mayor.

By the time we landed back on her doorstep, I was definitely feeling that this was more like a date than just dinner between friends. I felt my pulse increase. "I had a wonderful time tonight, Chase. Really. Dinner with you was better than any date I've been on in years, and not just because I got to eat my fill of barbecue." She laughed, but her words held a ring of truth to them.

"Actually, I had that same thought over dinner. And you should always go out with men who appreciate your appetite, it's not something you should have to be worried about."

"You're great Mayor Chase, you know that?" She didn't wait for me to respond, just wrapped her arms around me and pressed her lush, feminine curves against me as she squeezed tight. "Next time, dinner is on me." Then she kissed me, right on the cheek.

Totally platonic, which should have made it feel like the kiss of death.

Except it didn't.

It felt like a reason to hope.

Then again, maybe that was just wishful thinking.

CHAPTER 9
CARLOTTA

It was difficult to stand beside Chase inside The Old Country House barn after our non-date this past weekend.

It wasn't awkward or weird, but that goodbye hug and G-rated peck on the cheek felt charged. Sexually, and electrically charged. My heart had raced like crazy the whole time, and even after Chase had said goodnight, he filled my thoughts. Dirty thoughts. Sexy thoughts.

All around inappropriate thoughts.

But I was a professional, and today we were meeting for business. Well *I* was meeting for business, he was here as a favor to his sister. "I think this barn is perfect for what Pippa described as her dream wedding space, but without a tentative guest list, I can't say for certain."

"Why?" Chase looked around the now empty barn with a frown on his face. "This place seems massive."

"It is, but it will fit one hundred people, possibly one-fifty. But don't forget that the groom is a very famous rock star, which I'm guessing means a much larger guest list." I assumed there would be plenty of executives and agents and assistants invited to the event.

Chase shook his head. "It's a wedding, not a business meeting."

Those were my exact sentiments, but I'd been planning weddings, christenings, Mitzvahs, and everything else for years, from my experience, I knew that people with money often blurred the lines.

"You'd be surprised how many weddings were filled with business associates of the bride or the groom, and in a lot of cases, the parents of the bride and groom."

"Seriously?"

"Yes, unfortunately." I gave the barn one last look, because I could already see Pippa's vision coming together. This place with hay on the ground, a small dance floor inside and a larger covered one on the outside. Twinkle lights and sparkling ribbons hanging from the ceiling. It would be rustic and sophisticated, just as she wanted. If we could just get a tentative head count for the guest list.

"No offense, but all this seems so extravagant for a wedding."

"None taken," I assured him. "Weddings are meant to be extravagant and over the top. It's the one day you're allowed to do the most, and all in the name of celebrating your love." I was a romantic at heart, even though with each wedding I planned, I grew more certain that it wouldn't happen for me.

"That's one way to think about it. Another, is if you want the best chance of relationship success, take the wedding money and buy a house or invest it."

"How romantic," I said sarcastically, barely able to hide my eye roll.

"Maybe not romantic, but most relationships end because of communication or money problems. This eliminates at least one of those issues, and it's more romantic to stay together than get divorced isn't it?"

My lips curved into an unconscious smile. "When you're right, you're right, Mr. Mayor."

"Now we're talking." He smiled and gave the barn one final look before he followed me out. "What's next, invitations?"

My laugh echoed in the grassy field as we made our way towards the golf cart parked on the paving stones that lead to other parts of the property. "Today is strictly venues."

"*Only* venues? You said she wanted a barn."

I laughed at his accusatory tone. "She does, but Pippa still hasn't narrowed down her dates, and if this barn is booked by the time she decides, she'll need a backup venue."

"A backup venue." He said the words like they were a fatal disease diagnosis. "Okay," Chase sighed. "Where to next?"

"Here," I said with a smile and stopped the golf cart. "Margot calls this The Chapel, and it's a beautiful non-denominational church building with stained glass, cushioned wooden benches and everything a happy couple needs to get that church wedding feel."

Chase stepped out of the cart and came around to help me out, such a gentleman, before he turned to the building. "It's beautiful alright, a work of art, but why isn't a regular church good enough?"

"Most of the time, it is. But The Old Country House is meant to be a multi-functional event venue, so guests don't have to do a lot of traveling from the wedding to the reception, which only increases the cost for the person opening their wallet."

Usually it was the bride's family, but these days it was the whole family, or just the couple footing the bill. "And some couples who don't have a church or a pastor of their own don't want to jump through the hoops often required before a certain clergyman will perform the ceremony."

His brows furrowed. "Really?"

"Yes. Some require marriage counseling or proof of faith, all kinds of things. This is just to give our clients more options." And the space was so gorgeous many couples chose it without any religious bent to their wedding ceremony. "What do you think?"

"It's a work of art, like I said. Visually stunning, and would be good for pictures, I imagine. But if the barn might be too small, this is definitely too small."

I nodded. "Exactly what I hope you'll tell Pippa when she inevitably falls in love with the stained glass." Every bride fell in love with the space and tried to figure out how they could make it fit with their ideal wedding.

Chase's lips tugged to one side in a crooked grin. "I promise."

"The next space is off-campus. I'll drive." I headed back towards the golf cart when I realized Chase wasn't close. "What's wrong?"

"I thought the point of this space is so you don't need off-campus locations?"

I nodded. "That was the pitch made by Margot, not me. I'm an event planner, and I try to give my clients whatever they want that's within my power, even if that means leaving The Old Country House." Margot and I argued about it plenty, but it was unreasonable to expect every single bride to choose between her options, amazing though they were. "You coming?"

He nodded and grumbled something under his breath too low for me to hear, so I feigned ignorance. Eventually he joined me in the cart and we drove back to the main entrance where my Escalade was parked. "That's your car?"

I nodded. "Something wrong with it?"

Chase doubled over and laughed. "Not at all, it's just what is a little bitty thing like you doing driving the equivalent of a monster truck?"

I laughed. "It's hardly a monster truck, just bigger than the pickup trucks you boys are so fond of driving. Unlike those boys, my car serves a function. Lots of room for event cargo."

He eyed my car with great skepticism before turning his green gaze to me. "You need help getting in?"

"No, I have a step ladder in the backseat." I laughed at his shocked expression. "How little do you think I am Chase?"

He shrugged as a pink blush stained his cheeks. "Small enough that I believe there's a stool or ladder in the back to help you inside."

"Wanna bet on it?"

He thought about it for a long moment and then shook his head. "I'm learning not to bet against you Carlotta."

I flashed a satisfied smile. "That's because you're a very smart man, Mayor Chase. Hop in." Chase got into the vehicle much easier than I ever could, and I would have been impressed if I weren't so jealous. "Good job."

"Thanks," he smirked. "So where is this barn?"

I sighed, because this was the tricky part. "It's not

one hundred percent ready for prime time yet, but it can be done if Pippa chooses it." I cringed at my own words, because it was the worst thing a planner could say to a potential client. *Here's this great venue but it may or may not be available when you need it.*

"That doesn't tell me where it is."

I shook my head and wagged a finger at him. "Nothing gets past you, does it?"

"Very little," he admitted. "You're stalling."

I let out a shallow sigh and turned to Chase at a stop sign. "The property belongs to a family that has lived in Carson Creek for many years, possibly even generations. It's been, for all intents, vacant for a few years but it won't be for long."

"So you want my sister to get married in a dilapidated barn?"

"Of course not, but this barn is much larger, and I'll come out here myself to clean in my free time. I'll do it, if this is the best property for Pippa and Ryan's wedding." I glared at him and dared him to question me further.

"Seems excessive, but this is your job, not mine."

"Remember that," I told him and continued on to York Farm. Back in the day the place was filled with animals and children, and plenty of delicious food. These days, for the past decade or more really, it had basically been derelict. Abandoned and neglected. "We're here."

"York Farm?" Chase laughed. "This place hasn't been

up and running for years, and it'll take a lot more than a weekend or two of elbow grease to get it in working order."

I arched a brow and shifted my Escalade into park. "And you're so sure because of your vast experience farming or decorating?"

"Carlotta, for all you know, half the beams in that barn are rotten and need to be replaced." He shook his head and stared at me for a long moment before he hopped out and opened my door for me. "Be reasonable. Please."

"I'm always reasonable, Chase. Just because you're prone to panicking doesn't mean that this can't be done."

He gasped. "Prone to panicking? According to whom?"

I accepted his hand and slid from the car, my chin held high. "According to me, that's who."

"You're wrong," he insisted. "I don't panic. Almost never," he amended.

"Good, then you won't have a problem with me taking a tour of the barn for myself. Will you?" I folded my arms and dared him to add more oil to the current fire raging inside of me.

Chase held his hands up in a defensive gesture. "No problem for me. In fact, consider my lips sealed."

"Excellent. Come on." I forged ahead through the tall grass, not stopping until I spotted the reddish-brown barn in the middle of a field. It would look better with wild flowers growing all around, but beggars couldn't be choosers. "Wow," I sighed. The place was huge, at least double the size of the other barn.

I pulled out my phone to take photos, to capture everything I saw so that I could paint a picture for Pippa or my other clients. The barn boasted a thick layer of dust over everything, but despite that, I could see its potential.

"You're kidding," Chase said behind me, his voice thick with disbelief.

"Not kidding," I shot back, too busy taking photos to turn and see the look of skepticism I was sure was on his face. I got closer to the back of the barn, taking in every detail imaginable for later. Instead of watching where I was going, I focused on the image on my phone screen and kept snapping until my heel got stuck on a loose board. "Dammit." My arms flailed almost comically for several moments, a face plant was imminent.

Arms wrapped around me and startled me even worse than the potential fall and my arms flailed even more, sending me and the hard body that belonged to Chase tumbling to the ground. "Well that's a fine thank you," he said seconds after we hit the ground.

"Thanks," I groaned. "Much appreciated." Chase's lips twitched in good humor, and I realized how close we were in that moment. I could feel the quick pace of his heart against my chest, his firm abs against my squishy center, and what was behind his zipper pressed right up against me. "Really."

I tried to get up and fell twice more, landing on his hard muscles. His really hard body. "Carlotta..."

I growled in frustration. "Is it really necessary to be so hard? Everywhere?"

Chase laughed and his hands gripped my hips with a firm grasp to stop my movements.

I gasped and looked at him, which was a big mistake.

"Your squirming isn't helping."

"I know!" I tried to get up once again, using his chest to propel myself to my feet before falling back on top of him, giving the mayor a face full of perfume scented cleavage. "Sorry."

"Don't be," he murmured beneath me. "I'm fine..."

I don't know what it was about the moment that struck me as particularly funny, but I giggled. Then I couldn't stop laughing. Soon we both laughed and laughed, so much that I nearly forgot that I was smothering him with my breasts.

Nearly.

CHAPTER 10

CHASE

"Hold her closer Chase, she's not going to bite you." Pippa laughed at my discomfort holding the tiny bundle that was my niece in my arms. "She doesn't have any teeth yet."

"Funny," I growled at my sister, but did as she instructed, pulling Ryanna closer. I was hesitant at first, because she was so little, and I was worried I'd hurt her, but with her head nestled against my chest the little girl gave a hum of approval and instantly stopped squirming. "Hey, that worked!"

"Duh," she said and rolled her eyes as she poured two cups of coffee. "It's decaf."

"Why?" Decaf wasn't meant to be consumed, it was just a waste of coffee.

"Because some of us have to use our bodies to nourish the next generation, and caffeine isn't good for babies, if you haven't heard." She smirked and took a seat at the shabby chic kitchen table she'd recently sanded and painted herself.

"Oh. Right." I looked down at Ryanna and smiled again. There was something so sweet and innocent about a baby, so tiny and vulnerable, that all I wanted to do was protect her and make sure no harm ever came to her. "Sorry. How are you feeling?"

"Wonderful," she sighed. "But exhausted. Ryanna is a princess in the truest sense of the word. She wakes up when she feels like it without any regard to her poor, tired momma. She gets loud when she's hungry or grumpy or scared, or when she needs a fresh diaper."

I smiled and looked down at Ryanna, her big blue eyes studying me closely. "All I hear your momma saying is that you're just like her." She gurgled and I took it as agreement. "Yep, I know."

"Hilarious," Pippa said with an eyeroll I'd grown used to over the years. "So..." she began slowly.

"So," I shot back with a blank expression.

Pippa's lips pulled into a half-grin. "You're here to talk about wedding stuff."

"I am." My brows dipped in confusion. "You *did* ask me to help Carlotta with wedding stuff."

"I did."

"Okay. We looked at venues recently." Instead of reliving the feel of Carlotta's body pressed up against mine, her soft feminine curves that felt so good against the stark hardness of my own frame, I ran through each venue with my sister. "The off-site barn holds more people, but the Old Country House barn will better suit your wedding aesthetic. All Carlotta needs is a rough estimate of your guest list."

Pippa stared at me as if I was speaking a foreign language, which I kinda understood, because wedding speak was a foreign language to me, but this was her wedding.

"I have no idea honestly. Just book the bigger barn, I guess."

I bit back my frustration and stared at my sister. She did look exhausted, but this felt like something more. Maybe. I wasn't good at noticing details like inner turmoil.

"What's going on Pippa? You still want to get married, don't you?"

"Of course, I do. I love Ryan, and this is the start of the life we should have had." Her eyes went wistful for a moment as if she was thinking about all the years they'd lost together over a misunderstanding.

"But?"

"But I'm exhausted Chase. Ryanna is a lot more work than running a restaurant."

I blinked. "I should hope so, since the restaurant is full of professional and capable adults, and she is just a little baby." Ryanna's blue eyes sparkled as if she understood. "All you have to do is decide. And you should sleep when the baby sleeps."

"Who are you, and what have you done with my brother?"

I smiled. "A new baby in town is everybody's business Pip, and all the women in my office insist on passing me bits of advice for you. That's one that stuck. Don't try to do laundry or clean when she's asleep, just sleep with her. Makes sense now."

She smiled. "All right. Thanks, I think."

"The barn," I reminded her with a playful tone.

"I assume Carlotta is assuming plenty of Ryan's professional contacts will be invited, so tell her to book the bigger barn even if it is off-site, which will mean some kind of transportation from the hotels and B&Bs in town. And for food, I want Nina to do the food."

"Isn't she an employee of Dark Horse?"

"Yes, but I have an in with the owner. I'll just have to use certain methods of persuasion."

"Don't need to know, thanks. Just confirm and get back to me. Or Carlotta."

My sister's blue eyes studied me in much the same manner as my niece's had. "How are things going with Carlotta?"

"What do you mean?" Had Carlotta told her what happened at the barn? Did she feel that spark of attraction as I had and said something to Pippa? I doubted it, but dammit, was it normal to grow a sudden attraction for a woman I'd known forever?

"How are the wedding plans coming along?"

"Oh. Fine. Good. I'm just a go between, like a wedding planning conduit."

"Yeah? Because I heard you went on a date with Carlotta. Is there anything else I should know?"

"Nope," I answered quickly. Only then did I realize it was too quickly.

"Rrriiiight," she drew the word out to four syllables.

"It was just two friends having dinner," I assured my sister, or maybe I was just trying to assure myself. "It was a thank you, because she was able to find someone to build me shelves that I actually liked, and they did it on the weekend so my workday wouldn't get interrupted. It was worth a big thanks, I think." And it had led to the renewal of an unexpected friendship.

"Who did you call that couldn't build shelves over a weekend?"

I sighed. "I had asked CJ to take care of the task." At Pippa's skeptical look, I shrugged. "What? It seemed like something she could handle."

"She was probably hoping the inconvenience would mean working from the very private confines of your house. Some alone time, if you know what I mean." Just in case I didn't know what she meant, Pippa wiggled her brows, her insinuation a bit heavy handed.

"First of all, a blind person would know what you

mean, Pip. Second, you're wrong. CJ is a young woman and she's just eager to do a good job." I'd been the same way with my first job, and even during my first couple years as mayor. Over the top eager to prove myself, to prove to my fellow citizens they hadn't made a mistake by casting their vote for me.

"She's not that young," Pippa insisted, and I knew she was arguing for the sake of arguing. One of her favorite past times was to give me a hard time about my dating life, or lack of a dating life, I suppose.

"She's incredibly young Pippa."

"I don't know baby brother, Carlotta might say the same thing about you, but I'm guessing you both had a good time on your non-date?"

"Did she say that?" The question came out too eager, even to my ears.

"She hasn't said anything. Yet. But based on your reaction just now, I'm damn sure going to ask."

"Pip," I groaned. "It was just two friends having dinner."

"Yeah?"

"Yeah," I insisted, suddenly the defiant little brother who would do anything to prove his sister wrong.

She pointed a finger at me, a triumphant smile on her face. "Maybe you want to tell that to the blush coloring your cheeks tomato red." At my groan, she laughed and finished off that abomination she called coffee.

I stood and dropped a kiss on Ryanna's head. "Would you look at the time? I'm running late for...something."

Pippa laughed and followed me as I put her sleeping daughter in the playpen beside the kitchen. "You can't hide from me forever Chase, you know that."

"Not forever," I called over my shoulder. "Just for a while. Get some sleep," I told her and closed the front door behind me before she could say another word.

CHAPTER 11
CARLOTTA

"It's a little early in the day for you to be drinking, isn't it?" Grady stared down the length of his nose at me with a playful smirk. "Rough day?"

I sighed. "It's not even noon yet," I replied.

Grady only shrugged. "Look around Carlotta, this place isn't exactly empty, and it's not just because I make a mean pastrami on rye."

"On another day I'd be here to indulge, but I have a cake tasting today and I need all the room I can make in here." I patted my belly once and leaned back onto the bar, ignoring the way my stomach lurched at the idea that I'd be seeing Chase again. Soon. Really soon, and I couldn't handle it. I was a mass of nerves and anxiety, and even excitement, which was crazy. Totally crazy, I knew that, but my body wasn't working with the same goals as my head.

"Okay, so you've finally gotten up the courage to ask me out?"

"No," I laughed. "You're a looker for sure, but you don't want a woman like me, I'm too high maintenance for you."

"Maybe. Or maybe you're just trying to let me down easy." He winked to let me know he was just kidding.

"I'm actually here because I need you, Grady."

He leaned forward, resting on his tattooed forearms with a sultry smile. "I'm listening."

"I was wondering if you'd be up for bartending Pippa and Ryan's wedding? You might not want to work it, and I totally get that, but I was thinking maybe we'd just do a couple signature cocktails in addition to beer and champagne. Nothing too crazy, but you have a way with people, and you're used to handling tipsy folks, so I thought it'd be a natural fit." The words rushed out of me nervously, even though Grady hadn't given me any reason to worry.

"I get to keep the tips?"

I nod. "Of course. In addition to a flat rate for the day."

Grady shook his head and my shoulders slumped. This was a perfect plan for Ryan and Pippa's wedding. It would eliminate the need for drinks servers at the venue, which I still didn't have yet. "Keep the flat rate, and I'll work for tips. That'll be my gift to the happy couple."

I sat up taller and smiled. "You'd do that Grady?"

He nodded.

"How gracious," Margot appeared beside me and sneered. "Giving a rock star a hundred-dollar wedding present. It's probably more than you can afford."

I gasped at her rudeness. "Unnecessary Margo, and rude as hell."

"It's called sincerity Margot. If there wasn't a dark pit where your heart should be, you'd understand the concept." He turned to me and ignored the sharp gasp and look of hurt on Margot's face. "I'll even create the cocktails for 'em. Just give me some tips on what they like, and if I should do one of those mocktails for Pippa."

"That's a great idea!" I stood and reached over the bar to wrap one arm around Grady in a clumsy hug. "Thank you so much. I'll talk with Pippa and let her know! You're the best Grady."

"Don't you forget it," he drawled just as my phone vibrated with an alarm.

"I won't forget it," I told him. "Now it's cake time. See you later." I made my way outside, but not before I slid a pair of sunglasses over my eyes, and thank goodness I did, because Chase was already here, leaning against my truck, waiting for me. He looked good. No, he looked damn good, like one of those rom-com love interests. He was casually cool and stylish without really trying. The dark jeans fit his body perfectly, showing off the muscles he usually kept hidden, and a lightweight sweater that amplified his biceps. And pecs.

Enough! I shouted at my worked-up libido. "Hey."

"Hey," he said back, lips curling into a sexy, knowing smile. "You know, I'm not sure I will ever get used to the idea that you drive this thing."

I shrugged, but couldn't help smiling at his words. "Give it a few more trips and you'll get used to it. Hop in."

"I'll just step in because I am adult sized," he joked.

"Hey, petite is still adult sized! If anything, you're kind of a giant."

He laughed. "Are you trying to give me a complex so you can eat all the cake samples?"

"I hadn't thought of that, because I'm not that clever, but I've got my eye on you, Mr. Mayor. Who knew you could be so devious?"

We laughed together and enjoyed comfortable, amiable conversation until we reached Perfect Day Cakes. Pippa wanted to use Nina for the cake as well, but the chef had insisted that if she were getting married, she would go to Perfect Day Cakes as her number one pick. "Here we are."

"This is it? It seems so small," he said as he eyed the small store front with confusion.

"This isn't a traditional bakery. They specialize in

wedding cakes and other event desserts. The dining space in front is strictly for cake tastings."

Chase stepped from my truck easily and walked around to help me down with a gentle smile. He held a hand out and I took it, gasping at his strength and another zap of electricity that began where our hands were connected. "Is this a sustainable business model?"

I nodded. "Weddings are a very lucrative business, Chase. Isn't that how Margot convinced you to re-zone the space for multiple business purposes?"

"Well yes, but she sold me on weddings *and* other events. I didn't realize a business could survive on just weddings." He shook his head in disbelief and shut my door behind me, staying close beside me like a perfect southern gentleman.

"They cater predominantly to weddings, but there are other events like anniversary parties, divorce parties, and even cakes to celebrate retirement. It's never *just* weddings."

Chase absorbed my words and nodded, while I steered us towards the front door. Perfect Day Cakes had a simple décor of off-white and light blue, black & white wedding cake photos on the walls, and the chairs and tables were set up like the bride and groom's table. "Adorable," I cooed just as the owner, Madeline, rushed out with a grin.

"Carlotta and Chase, I presume?"

I nodded. "I'm Carlotta Montgomery, the wedding

planner. Thank you for getting us in on such short notice."

Madeline grinned. "My husband and my brothers are huge fans of TGB and I'm a big fan of new clients, so here we are. I have six cakes prepared for you to taste. Are we ready?" Before we could answer, Madeline led us to a small table in the middle of the dining room. "Sparkling water will help keep your palates clean between cakes." With those words, she disappeared behind swinging metal doors.

I leaned back in my chair and removed my sunglasses. "Pippa didn't give you any guidance?" The woman was oddly removed from her own wedding planning, which was worrisome, except I knew Pippa and how excited she was to marry Ryan.

"She said nothing weird like blue cheese frosting. No jams or jellies between the cake layers, and she'd be up for some type of bacon flavor in the frosting, but she gets final approval on that." He rolled his eyes. "I think she just wants to taste bacon maple frosting."

The first cake was a lemon cake with a Limoncello buttercream frosting. It was heavenly, but boring. "So?"

"Delicious, but a little lowkey for a wedding, don't you think?"

I smiled and nodded. "Agreed."

"This cake," Madeline began with a proud smile. "Is Amaretto Orange with an apricot mousse between the layers."

Chase tasted it first, and the way he moaned in appreciation was so erotic I had to slam my knees shut against the pulsing between my thighs. "Damn, that is divine. Literally divine."

After that endorsement, how could I not? I slid my fork through the slice and pushed it between my lips. It was divine. It was beyond divine. I looked to Madeline. "Are you some kind of witch?"

She laughed. "I prefer sorceress, but that's my business."

The red velvet cake was delicious, but mostly forgettable after that Amaretto magic.

"That's stunning!" I practically yelled when the red wine cake came out. "The color alone will win Pippa over."

"Let's hope the taste will too," Madeline said and stepped back, giving us privacy to taste her creation.

It was wonderful. Sweeter than I would have imagined for red wine cake, but moist and creamy and utterly delicious. "That is fabulous."

"It's so good," Chase said around a bite and leaned forward to stop the frosting from falling, but he was too late. One drop hit his sweater, his cream-colored sweater, and his hand went to spot instinctively and he rubbed it in before I could tell him not to. "Dammit."

"Stop! You're smearing it in Chase, and the stain will set."

His broad shoulders fell, and I couldn't help but smile. "It's ruined."

"It's not," I insisted. "I'll take the sweater home with me and fix it right up for you." I stood just as Madeline came out again.

"Is there a problem?"

"Yes. Your red wine cake is so delicious that Chase decided to wear it."

"Funny," he growled, and even that sound slid down my spine and turned my legs into a puddle of goo, which should have warned me to back away, to give him my fabric stain pen and go about my day.

"I'm sorry about the stain, but I'm thrilled you loved it. Please don't go just yet," she begged and rushed away once again.

"I can't sit here with a giant stain Carlotta, I have afternoon meetings today."

"Fine. Go hide out in the car while I finish up here." I offered Chase my keys and shooed him out the door, because goodness gracious, the man could short circuit a brain without even trying. It really wasn't fair, just as it wasn't fair that I was suddenly noticing that the good mayor was a man. A big, fine, delicious man.

Madeline returned with a sheepish smile. "I overheard you talking about bacon, sorry-not-sorry for eavesdropping, and I thought this might be up your bride's alley. It's devil's food cake with whiskey, maple bacon frosting. Take it to go," she insisted and handed me the bag. "There's a big slice for the bride as well."

I smiled. "I like the way you think Madeline, and I think you and I are going to have a wonderful working relationship."

"Fingers crossed," she said and waved me off.

The ride back to my place was mostly quiet but companionable, both of us lost in our thoughts, and much of mine were centered on the man beside me. Was this just hormones? Too much time passed without sex? Without being held by a man? Or was this worse, was it genuine attraction to man I'd known most of my life? I didn't know, which was unique for me, and I shook off the desire—tried to anyway—and focused on the job at hand.

I was a professional event planner, and that's what this is, a job. An important job, at that. One I couldn't afford to ignore in favor of a brief fling or whatever was going on between me and Chase.

Without a word we both got out of the car and walked the stone path from my driveway to my house. As soon as we were inside, I made a mad dash for the laundry room, and ran right into Chase on my way, well, back to Chase.

"Sorry," I said, and I might have said more, but the feel of his hand, big, strong and hot on my waist distracted me. "Take off your shirt."

He frowned until I pointed to the big deep red stain

over his right pec. "Oh. Right. Sorry." He didn't need to be sorry, but I knew I would be when he tugged the sweater over his head with one hand to reveal nothing more than a white tank top that—hot damn—showed off every inch of muscle in his arms and shoulders. "Here you go." Chase held the shirt out to me and I blinked once, twice, maybe five times until I could see something other than his muscles.

"Right. Thanks." I yanked the shirt from his grip and sought refuge in the laundry room. What right did he have, did any man have, to look so delicious in nothing but a tank? It wasn't right, and it wasn't fair, and I took all of my annoyance, and sexual frustration, out on that wine stain until the dark color started to lighten. "Okay. Good. You'll be all right," I muttered to the stain and took three deep breaths before exiting the laundry room again.

When I got to the kitchen I stopped dead in my tracks. Chase was shirtless, completely and totally naked from the waist up. His back was expansive, and every move he made over the kitchen sink showed me different muscles in a new light.

"What are you doing?"

He turned quickly, and as much as I was enjoying the view, I really wished he would have kept his back to me, because the front was equally delicious. He had a light smattering of auburn hair that didn't hide his small waist, six-pack abs or those dark peach nipples. He was, in a word, magnificent.

"There was some wine on my undershirt too," he said sheepishly. "Is that okay?"

I kept staring, because when was the last time I saw such a gorgeous man up close and personal like this?

Never, my mind filled in the blanks.

"Carlotta?"

I blinked and shook my head. "Yeah?" The word came out breathless and a bit needy.

"You're staring."

I nodded my agreement. "You're shirtless and...hot."

He smiled. "Thanks?"

"Why?" I marched across the kitchen and poked him in the chest. "Why are you...why is this? Why are we...?" I couldn't even form a coherent sentence, and it only made me madder so I poked his chest again.

Chase grabbed my wrist to stop the poking and pulled me in close, so close that I could see the stubble sprouting on his shaved jaw.

"I don't know either," he said with a smile before his lips met mine in a splendid kiss that was so hot I thought my house would go up in flames with us still in it. His mouth moved, strong and capable, demanding and firm, but just enough that I could pull back if I wanted.

Not that I could even if I'd wanted to. The kiss was exactly what a kiss should be, and I wanted more. I wrapped my arms around his massive shoulders and I pressed myself against him fully, letting the hardness of his masculine form make me feel like a woman.

Chase's hand went to my backside and squeezed.

I moaned.

He moaned in response and gripped me harder, lifting me in the air. He released a low hum of approval when my legs wrapped around his waist.

I gasped in his mouth at the feel of him between my thighs, hot and hard—really, really hard—pressed to my core. We kissed right there in my kitchen for an eternity, nibbling and biting and tasting and teasing each other. His hips moved ever so slightly, increasing the pressure of his erection behind his zipper.

"Chase," I moaned against his lips and moved my hips.

His grip tightened and he pressed me against the fridge, allowing me to feel more of his hardness. So. Much. More.

A ringing sound pierced the air, but I didn't pull back, didn't stop, didn't even care. Neither did Chase apparently, because eventually the ringing stopped. But we didn't.

The ringing started again, and Chase's shoulders fell. "We should probably be responsible adults right now."

"Probably," I agreed with a disappointed sigh.

"It's the right thing to do," he said with a small smile.

"Definitely that," I agreed again. And then, I surprised myself by cupping his face and kissing him again. I nibbled his lips and sucked on his tongue until I was sure he would strip me out of my clothes and give us what we both wanted, right there in my kitchen.

But the damn phone rang. Again.

Chase growled. "I'll get it." He waited until my feet were on the floor to step back and reach for his phone on the counter, groaning when he looked at the screen. "My assistant. I have to go."

I did the only thing I could, nodded at his words. "I'll give you a ride back to your car."

"No thanks," he grinned. "I should probably walk off the effects of you before my meeting." Without another word of whether or not we would pick up from that kiss later, Chase left.

Damn him, he left and I was still here, hot and bothered.

And hoping for more.

CHAPTER 12
CHASE

Who knew one little kiss could bring a grown man to his knees?

I've been kissed before, plenty of times if you want to get down to the truth of the matter. Sure, I was a nice guy. A good guy. The perfect southern gentleman who opened doors for women and pulled their chairs out for them, but when it came right down to it, I was your average red-blooded American male who appreciated beautiful women and hot bodies. And no one was hotter than Carlotta Montgomery two days ago in the middle of her kitchen.

She smelled like flowers and earth, like vanilla and magic, sex and mystery. Everything about the woman was a conundrum. She was prim and proper, a real lady, but the way she'd kissed me in her kitchen, pushed her curves against me and moaned into my mouth, was *not* what one expected from a prim and proper southern belle. The way she rolled her hips and growled her pleasure was seared into my mind, tattooed in my memories for all of eternity.

I couldn't even say what happened. One moment she was staring at me from the other side of the kitchen, eyes glazed over with recognizable lust, lips slightly parted. The temperature in the room had cranked up, and the next thing I knew our bodies were fused together, seeking bone-deep pleasure with nothing but our mouths.

Okay, not *just* our mouths. Every single time I closed my eyes, all I could see was her legs wrapped around me, the warmth of her core cradling what I thought was an unfortunate erection. Only, instead of being offended or upset, Carlotta was into it. She'd ground against me, gave herself more and more pleasure at my expense. It was a heady experience, having a beautiful woman like Carlotta Montgomery using me like a scratching post and I wasn't mad about it.

My only regret is that I didn't stay long enough to see what came next, because I was sure that there was more to come.

"Hello? Chase, are you even listening to me?" CJ stood in front of my desk with her hands fisted on her hips and a scowl on her face as if she were *my* boss. "Well?"

I blinked and bit back my frustration that once again

my assistant was ruining my fantasies of Carlotta. "What is it, CJ?"

"Oh nothing," she shrugged in that mock casual way that some women did when they wanted attention. I smiled to myself. *Maybe Pippa wasn't so far off base, after all.* "Just me trying to make sure you're prepared for today's meeting. Nothing important. At all."

"Isn't that your job?"

The question took her by surprise. "Well yes, which is why you should be listening instead of daydreaming."

I leaned back in my chair, wondering if CJ was becoming a little too casual in her approach to our working relationship. "I'm listening now. What were you saying?"

CJ paused for a quick second, unsure how to respond to my recalcitrant tone. "The old auto factory on the northwest edge of town is dilapidated and in need of an investor."

"I'm aware." I'd been working for the past year to entice some company to take over the building, turn it into something new and revive the stagnating industrial employment in the area.

"Well, the potential owners are interested. Extremely interested, Chase. But they want a reason to stay here, a reason to choose Carson Creek." She leaned forward and I averted my gaze to her youthful face. "Give them a reason."

"Thank you, CJ." I knew what she was getting at, but

tax breaks were no way to lure in potential business unless pleasing the rich overlords was your only concern. "I'll take those words under advisement. Anything else?"

Her brows dipped in confusion. "Well no, I just figured you'd want the down-low on what they're after."

"And you've given it to me. Thank you."

She nodded, still unsure of my firm tone. "You're welcome?" I didn't say a word and CJ leaned in closer. "Did I do something wrong, Chase?"

"No, not at all. Why?"

She straightened and took a step back. "No reason. You seem irritable today, that's all. Should I reschedule the meeting? Or maybe you'd like it if I attended the meeting with you since I've been dealing with them for the past month and a half."

"No thanks. You stay here and make sure nothing essential escapes my notice."

"Okay," she nodded. "Maybe I should swing by before dinner so we can get your notes from the meeting jotted down. You know, while they're fresh in your memory." Dammit, Pippa was right. I would have to say something, or do something to dissuade CJ from whatever it was she was attempting.

"That's a good idea, but not tonight. I have plans."

"You do? No plans are on the schedule."

I smiled patiently. "That's because these are personal plans, the kind you don't have your assistant set up for you. When you're done at five, you can clock out and enjoy the rest of your evening, CJ. You're young, go out and have fun or take selfies. Whatever it is young adults your age do for fun."

"You could come out with me and see for yourself."

"I could, but that would be highly inappropriate, wouldn't it?"

CJ shook her head with a sigh. "I'd call it improving our working relationship."

Of course she would. "Not tonight." I had plans tonight that included Carlotta, even though she didn't know it yet.

"Okay," she shrugged like it was no big deal, but I could see the disappointment in her eyes and the set of her shoulders. "Then I guess I'll see you tomorrow. Good luck with your meeting."

I flashed a wide but professional smile. "Thank you CJ, for all of your hard work."

"Uh, no problem. I'm always here to help if you need me." She waited for me to say something, anything else, and when it became clear that I had nothing else to say, she turned and sauntered out of my office with all the fanfare of a visiting dignitary.

Alone again, I let my thoughts wander back to Carlotta and my plans for the evening.

My plans for her.

CHAPTER 13
CARLOTTA

Living alone as a single woman in the twenty-first century meant a girl could never be too cautious. I kept a bat beside my bedroom door, pepper spray on my keychain near the front door, and I had years of self-defense training under my belt. So, when the doorbell rang after nine o'clock in the evening, I went on full alert.

There was no good reason anyone would stop by at this hour without notice. Usually this meant a medical emergency, death, or worse, a wedding emergency. I stood and paused the singing competition I was barely paying attention to and sighed before I made my way to the door. Heart racing, I slid in front of the peephole, my breath hitched at the sight of Chase on my doorstep.

Chase? What is he doing here?

There was only one way to find out, so I sighed again

and looked down at my outfit with a critical eye. Rainbow farting unicorns danced on my pajama pants, and the plain white tank I had on wasn't exactly appropriate for company of the male variety. Then again Chase hadn't said anything about our kiss a few days ago, so did it really matter?

Only one way to find out.

With another sigh to calm my racing heart, I opened the door with a smile. "Chase. Hey." It wasn't the smoothest or sexiest greeting, but it was all I could muster.

"Hey," he said back with an almost shy smile that was absolutely irresistible. "Sorry to swing by unannounced. Do you have a minute to talk?"

To talk. Of course he wanted to talk, and good money said the topic of conversation would be that hot kiss that replayed on a nonstop loop in my mind. I took a step back to wave Chase inside.

"Sure. What's up?" There, that sounded calm and cool, like a sophisticated woman who would deal with this man, *any* man, without turning into a babbling fool.

"What's up?" Chase sucked in a deep breath and released it slowly as he scrubbed a hand down his face. "We should talk. About the kiss."

I smiled tightly, because the tense set of his shoulders, the frown lines he couldn't hide around his mouth, told me this was the, *it was a mistake and can't happen again* conversation. "What about it?"

"For starters, it was pretty unexpected." His lips quirked into a grin that transformed his expression from a scowl to a heated gaze. "It wasn't an unwelcomed experience, but it did catch me off guard."

"Same," I agreed. "I wasn't expecting it, but it was one heck of a kiss." There was no point beating around the bush or trying to play cool, not when my entire body had been wrapped around his while I rubbed against his hard erection. "Are you here for a repeat or a reproach?"

Chase's shoulders fell, and I tried to talk my traitorous body down from the edge of lust. "I don't know, honestly. I haven't been able to stop thinking about that kiss, and the way your body felt pressed against mine. What do you think that means?"

I couldn't help but smile at his clinical approach to a scorching hot encounter. Chase was adorable sure, but he was unintentionally sexy as well, and now that he was here in my house, forcing me to talk about that kiss, I knew exactly what I wanted. I took one step closer and then another.

"I think it probably means that you want to kiss me again."

His nostrils flared. "And again." Those two little words came out on a low growl as he bridged the gap between us and speared one hand through my hair as the other gripped my hip and brought our bodies flush together. "And again," he whispered a moment before his lips were on mine, ravishing me, devouring every inch of my mouth until I was hot and dizzy.

My arms instinctively went around his neck, and I pressed myself against him, tempting him, or maybe I was teasing him. Possibly even daring him. Chase's mouth was magical as his tongue slipped between my lips and danced with my own. He tasted of coffee and chocolate, and I wanted more. A lot more. "Chase," I panted.

He growled low and deep, a guttural sound that reverberated through me and shook my spine like fork tines. Heat suffused my skin as his mouth left mine and left a trail of heat across my throat. His nibbled a line of fire from my earlobe to my shoulder, sliding my spaghetti strap down and kissing that specific spot.

"You're so beautiful Carlotta."

Beautiful. It was something I hadn't been called in ages, and my body flamed with arousal. "Right now, I feel beautiful."

Chase stepped back and looked at me, his green eyes so dark and piercing my core clenched. With one finger he hooked the spaghetti strap on my left arm through his finger and put it back where it was before doing the same on the right. His hands skimmed down my waist and stopped at the hem of my shirt, and in the next moment he lifted it over my head and tossed it behind him. "So fucking beautiful."

I don't know if it was his gaze or hearing that word

come from his mouth, but my nipples hardened instantly. His mouth caught one hard nipple between his teeth and nibbled. And nibbled. When I was practically vibrating with need, he sucked it into his mouth and I cried out in pleasure. "Chase, yes!"

He kissed and licked his way across the small valley between my breasts and tortured me some more. His big strong hands gripped my breasts, kneading one while he feasted on the other. My fingers slipped between his wavy red hair and held him close because he was right where I needed him in that moment.

Until his lips traveled lower and he released my breasts to put his hands on my pants. "Nice pajamas," he grinned up at me with a gleam in his eye.

"Thanks. I wasn't expecting company."

"I like 'em. They make you less intimidating."

I smiled at that. "Little ol' me? Intimidating? Hardly."

His deep chuckle released a gust of air on the strip of skin just above my waistband. And then his fingers were there between my flesh and my pajamas as he tugged them down, my boring black panties along with them. "Black lace, of course," he growled and gripped one thigh to toss it over his shoulder.

Oh goodness gracious yes! I hadn't been with a man in so long I was self-conscious in the way women can be when a man is about to devour them. But one touch from his mouth, and all I could focus on was the feel of his cold, wet tongue on my swollen clit. Chase really did have a talented mouth, every swipe of his tongue, every little nibble on my most sensitive flesh only intensified my desire for him. For more. "Chase," I panted because I was embarrassingly close to orgasm.

He hummed his approval and tugged my clit between his lips and teeth, and the vibrations combined with the feel of his stubbled jaw on my inner thigh sent me over the edge. Quickly. I shook as the orgasm worked its way to the surface and shot out of my body like a rocket.

"Chase."

He looked up at me and I stared down at his unwaveringly masculine and utterly satisfied grin, evidence of my pleasure all over his glistening lips. "How's that for a kiss?"

I laughed and cupped his face, pulling him up to kiss him again. It wasn't something I'd ever done or ever been comfortable doing, but in this moment it felt right. Oh, so right. While we kissed, I undid his button and zipper, eagerly shoving his pants and boxer briefs down his thighs and stroked his hot, hard length. "Wow."

He smiled against my mouth and pushed his hips against my hand. "You sure about this?"

I nodded against his mouth and returned his smile as my hand continued to stroke the soft flesh that contained his rock-hard erection. I pulled back and looked at him. "I need you, Chase. Now." Without thinking, I jumped up and wrapped my legs around his waist.

He growled and his big hands gripped the backs of my thighs, making me feel small in his arms. "I can't wait another moment," he whispered in my ear and slowly lowered my body onto his.

"Yes!" What happened next, I couldn't exactly say. It was a whirlwind of activity, right there in my front hall, up against the wall that separated the hall from the living room. His hips moved like a machine in quick, deep thrusts that ratcheted up my pleasure to a thousand. His sexy grunts and moans sent shivers throughout my body, and when his teeth sank into the sensitive skin between my neck and shoulder, I thought I'd died and gone to heaven.

Two orgasms in one night, and I closed my eyes in bliss, this second orgasm was a slow, burning release. But Chase wasn't done. His gaze seared into mine as he pumped harder and faster, chasing his pleasure as I pulsed around him and moisture flooded between us. "Carlotta." He growled and stilled for a long intense moment before his eyes slammed shut and his body shook with pleasure. "Carlotta," he sighed one final time, pressing his chest against mine as he claimed my mouth in another hot kiss.

"That was...amazing."

He smiled, but it wasn't cocky or even satisfied, it was almost affectionate. "It was pretty amazing, wasn't it?" His shock mirrored my own, and then he laughed nervously. "You're not just beautiful Carlotta, you're hot as hell."

I smiled and shook my head. "I'm all right," I told him easily. I knew what I was, and what I wasn't. I was pretty on a good day with makeup and the right outfit to show off my assets, but I wasn't truly beautiful in that way that some women are, naturally and confidently beautiful.

"If you really believe that, then I guess it's up to me to show you that you are a hell of a lot more than *all right*."

With those words he hooked an arm around my waist and carried me to my bedroom.

CHAPTER 14
CHASE

She was so damn beautiful my eyes watered just looking at her spread out on the bed, well-loved with flushed skin and hard nipples. Carlotta was a fantasy come to life. She reached out to me and smiled.

"You're too far away."

I took a step closer and she sat up, her hands gripped my shirt and pushed it up my chest and over my head until it was on the floor behind me.

"Better?"

"Getting there," she purred as her hands roamed over my chest and back and abs, her appreciative gaze and soft fingers had me getting hard again already. "You are magnificent Chase." The note of awe in her voice made my cock twitch towards her and her smile widened. She fisted my cock in her small hand, her big brown eyes never looking away from me as she stroked me, watching to see what I liked, which was easy, because when it came to her I liked everything.

"Carlotta," I groaned when she gripped me tighter and tugged me harder.

"Mmm, I'm right here," she moaned and flicked her tongue over the tip of my cock, laughing prettily when my hips bucked. A moment later she had me in her mouth, tongue and lips providing the perfect amount of moisture and pressure to send me over the edge soon. She hummed again around my erection as her free hand slid up my thigh to cup my sac.

"Carlotta," I growled. "Keep that up and this will be over too soon."

She laughed again and took me deeper, swallowing around me with a satisfied sound that sent vibrations through me.

For the rest of my life, I would never forget the way she looked up at me while she brought me to the brink of pleasure with her mouth. The way her eyes sparkled with satisfaction and triumph each time she pulled a reaction from me. It was the hottest damn thing ever, and when I gripped her hair, she growled and took me a fraction deeper. "Carlotta," I growled and pumped into her mouth.

Her response? To grip my ass and push me deeper.

It was hot. Incredibly hot, and I was about to pop off again. Way too soon. I took a step back, chest heaving with exertion and ecstasy. "Come here." I took her hand

and helped her onto her feet, twirled her around and bent her over the bed. She was tight as ever when I entered her from behind, pussy slick and pulsing around me. "Oh, babe."

She arched her back and I was a goner, smacking that perfectly round ass while I pumped my hips with the fierceness of a big cat claiming his woman because that's what she felt like in that moment. Mine. "Oh yes, Chase. Yes!" Her hips began to roll and moan after moan dripped from her mouth.

I was no virgin, but this right here with Carlotta? It was the best sex of my life. She was bold and didn't hesitate to reach out for her pleasure or mine. She was loud and not shy about it, which only turned me on more.

"More, Chase. Harder," she panted.

I gave her everything she asked for and more, holding her with one hand as I plunged into her over and over again until her arms buckled and she fell face first against the mattress. I took advantage and knelt on the bed, the angle sending me even deeper.

"Oh god!" That was it, all she said before her body gave up more pleasure. She shook and trembled, her hands fisted in her bedding as her teeth sank into that bottom lip.

I fell over the edge right after her, so close it was damn near simultaneous. I was lost in her sweet body, in the pleasure that fogged my brain and left my gaze slightly unfocused.

Eventually I fell to the bed and wrapped her in my arms. "I'm going to dream about you," I told her as my eyes fluttered shut.

Carlotta laughed. "If I let you sleep long enough to dream."

I smiled, wondering how in the hell I'd gotten lucky enough that a fine woman like her wanted me, of all people, to share her bed.

I never did get around to dreaming about her.

CHAPTER 15
CARLOTTA

It was time. I had given Pippa plenty of time to make some decisions about her wedding day, including the actual date of the event, and she'd done nothing. No, that wasn't exactly true, she'd done less than nothing. Weeks of planning, of securing a wedding cake maker, a venue, invitations and the like, and still I had no solid date to reserve anything.

Not one darn thing.

I stood on the doorstep of the surprisingly average home that Pippa shared with Ryan when he was in town, and rapped as hard as my knuckles could handle on the door. Pippa was a new mother and I respected that, the time and the effort it took to care for an infant, especially on her own, was inconceivable. But I needed answers and I wasn't leaving until I got them.

The door opened, and there he was, Chase, frowning at me as if I was some kind of interloper.

"Carlotta? What are you doing here?"

I ignored the way my belly lurched and the way my skin instantly flamed with heat at the sight of him.

Why? Because Chase, for all of his southern gentleman ways, all his polite manners and that *aww, shucks I'm such a nice guy* appeal, he was no different than any other scoundrel on the street. Five days had passed since he'd rocked my world and I hadn't heard neither hide nor hair from him. It didn't matter how handsome he looked in today's mayoral getup of gray pinstriped slacks and slush pink dress shirt that somehow made his pale skin look sun-kissed. None of it mattered, not to me anyway.

"Is Pippa around?"

He blinked at my abrupt tone and stepped back with a nod. "Everything all right?"

I ignored him once again and marched inside to confront my sort-of client. "Pippa, we need to talk."

She looked up from her fussy baby with big blue eyes full of confusion. "Carlotta. This is a nice surprise. I think." I understood her confusion and I took responsibility for a good chunk of it. Out of respect for her status as a new mom, I'd given her plenty of leeway, made tons of excuses, but that was all in the past. "What's up?"

"What's up," I repeated her words with as much patience as I could muster. "What's up is that I can't keep making plans for your wedding without a clear-cut date of when that wedding is actually supposed to take place. Set a date, right here and now, or I'm done planning this until you do." I felt bad doing it this way, especially in the face of her obvious exhaustion, but in time Ryanna would sleep through the night, wouldn't need to feed so often, her problems would lessen. Mine, however, would not. She looked at me with wide, shocked eyes. "I'm sorry but you need to at least provide basic details, and we needed those details yesterday." I folded my arms while she rocked the fussy baby in her arms, I tapped my foot impatiently for good measure. I knew Pippa, she was as stubborn and own-way as they come, but I wasn't going to let her wiggle out of dealing with this. The "this" being her own wedding.

Pippa looked at me, and then her brother as he re-entered the living room, and pouted. "Are you two ganging up on me?" Her eyes started to well with unshed tears, but she wasn't the first bride to hide behind tears. I knew all their tricks.

I aimed a freshly manicured nail in her direction and shook my head. "That's not going to get you out of anything this time, Pip." I started to pace as my frustration—at my bride-to-be and her brother—took hold. "*I* told you to wait until you settled into motherhood, but *you* insisted. *You* requested a big southern wedding that you have zero time or energy to plan. So, do you want to get married in two months, or next summer? What will it be?"

I can feel Chase's gaze boring a hole into the side of my face, willing me, almost daring me to glance in his direction, but I refused. I wasn't here to talk personal details, this was strictly a business call.

Finally, Pippa showed signs of life. She got up from the sofa and shoved Ryanna into my arms. The little girl was beautiful, if a little fussy, and instinctively I slowly rock her back and forth. "You don't understand Carlotta, I'm so tired all of the time, and most of the time I can hardly string together a sentence or remember what needs to be done, never mind plan wedding details."

With Ryanna in my arms, I did my best to keep my voice even and calm. "I do understand Pippa, which is exactly why I'm giving you the chance right now to choose a wedding date, or postpone it." Usually, I was a little kinder with paying clients, but Pippa had pushed the limits of my patience over the past few weeks. And sure, maybe I blamed her just the teensiest bit for what happened with me and Chase.

Pippa nodded, her gaze fixed on the floor as she matched my movements, pacing the length of the expansive living room. "Last weekend in July. Does that work?"

I nod as I mentally pictured the calendar in my head. "Yes. Two months is a tight fit, but it's definitely doable.

Was that so hard?" I smiled to soften the blow of my words and my previous ranting.

Pippa's shoulders sank. "No, it wasn't. I'm sorry."

I waved off her apology, because I didn't need to place blame, I needed details. "It's in the past as of right now. Moving on, did you like any of the cakes?"

She stopped pacing and nodded eagerly, a tired smile spread across her pretty face. "I really, really loved the whiskey, maple bacon cake. It was everything I want for my wedding, a little bit country and rock & roll, and a little sophisticated. But I'm worried, do you think it's too trendy for Carson Creek?"

"Pippa, sweetheart, this is your wedding. There's no such thing as too trendy, and you're a trendy kind of girl. Your wedding should be what *you* want, not what everyone thinks you should have. You and Ryan have waited too long for this day to care one whit about what anyone else thinks. They'll come and cry over the romance of it all, drink your booze and gobble up the cake no matter what." It was a variation of my standard speech when brides began to worry too much about what the guests would think of this or that detail, but I held my breath anyway, and waited for my words to sink in.

Pippa thought long and hard about it while I rocked Ryanna back and forth, and gave her head a tiny sniff. "The whiskey bacon maple cake and the amaretto cake, but in cupcake form. Is that okay?"

"More than okay," I assured her as I pulled out my phone with my free hand and made a voice note to connect with Madeline later today on the cake details. "What," I asked when I caught Pippa and Chase sharing identical expressions of surprise aimed at me.

"Nothing," Pippa insisted with a shake of her head, a small smile on her face. "You're so good at that, multitasking with a baby in your arms. Can you pretty, please teach me your magic?"

I chuckled. "She's so tiny and precious, and so well-behaved, it's easy. Plus, she smells amazing, and it keeps me calm."

"Ha!" Pippa guffawed, startling the baby, but she quickly settled. "Don't let that sweet face fool you, she's been fussy for the past two hours and now she's so content. Why? What's your secret?"

I shook my head and looked down at Ryanna. She was so small and beautiful, and I wondered if I'd ever get the chance to have a baby of my own. "Big boobs," I told her with a laugh. "They're like sleeping pills for babies."

"Sorry kiddo, I can't help you there." Pippa laughed at her words that little Ryanna couldn't understand. "I'm really sorry Carlotta."

"I know, and if you really want to make it up to me, give me something I can work with. Colors? Type of flowers? Anything, please."

She nodded and closed her eyes. "I can do this." I gave her a few minutes to gather her thoughts, because I knew Pippa, like most women, had been thinking about her perfect wedding day for many, many years. "Okay. All right," she sighed. "For colors I was thinking simple and elegant, white, gold and silver. For everything from the wedding party to the invitations and décor. Does that help?"

"Tremendously." With a wedding date, cake choice and a color scheme, I could get quite a bit done and quickly. "Thanks Pippa and I'm sorry I had to come down so hard on you, but it needed to be done."

"Obviously," she laughed and shook her head. "We're good, right?"

"Totally. This is business honey, and not at all personal, I just needed to give you a little shake." My phone vibrated in my back pocket and I rolled my eyes, because it couldn't possibly be good news, since bad news—Chase—was still staring at me. I picked it up in my most professional voice. "This is Carlotta." I held my breath and listened to Margot's worried concerns.

"Carlotta, the Wickham bride is having quite the fit. She's three months pregnant and the couture designer who made her dress refuses to *ruin the silhouette* by expanding it for her pregnant belly. Can you believe it? I need you to work your magic or the wedding isn't going to happen."

I closed my eyes and pinched the bridge of my nose. This could not be happening, not today. "This wedding is next weekend Margo."

"I know, and that's exactly why she called me, to talk you into doing this huge favor for her. And for us if you really think about it." I didn't need to hear her long-winded rationale, because we both knew I would do everything in my power to avoid delaying a wedding date.

"I'll make some calls, just tell her that she has to be willing to travel to a seamstress who can re-fit the gown." I ended the call with a sigh and turned to Pippa. "I have to go put out another fire, but I'll get back to you soon for more details."

Pippa nodded and sent me an odd look I couldn't decipher, even if I had time to think about it, which I didn't. "You know where to find me."

I nodded absently and pressed a soft kiss to Ryanna's head. "I'll see you later, Princess. Sleep well." I handed the baby back to her mother and rushed away without a word to Chase, who seemed equally content to avoid me. My heels clicked on the hard wood floor as I hurried towards the front door and down the stone driveway.

"Carlotta, wait up!" Chase's breathless voice sounded behind me, but like the angry coward I was, I quickened my step towards my truck.

CHAPTER 16
CHASE

For a second I thought Carlotta would continue on without acknowledging me, but a few feet from her pearl monster, she stopped and turned to me. Her brown eyes held no emotion, her bland expression was unreadable.

"What is it, Chase?"

Her cool greeting didn't bode well for me, so I nodded absently and waited for her eyes to connect to mine. "How are you, Carlotta?"

"I'm doing good Chase. How are you?" Her stiff, formal tone took me further off guard and my shoulders sank in disappointment.

"I'm good. Look, did I do something wrong?"

She shrugged off the question as if it was ridiculous. "What could you have possibly done wrong? I mean, I haven't seen you since you slipped from my bed in the middle of the night, what could you have done?" She tapped her chin, and she did it sarcastically if that was possible.

"I didn't," I insisted but it felt silly even to my ears. "Okay maybe I did, but it was only because I didn't think you'd want people to see me leaving your house at that hour." I knew that was a legitimate answer, but Carlotta wasn't buying it.

One perfectly sculpted brow arched in skepticism and her lips pulled into a tight smile that wasn't really a smile. "I think maybe it was *you* who didn't want to be seen leaving my place at such a *suggestive* hour." Her knowing tone was so smug, so all-knowing that I wanted to lie just to prove her wrong.

"Okay, maybe that's true, but it's not for the reasons you might think." I didn't know how to explain it without sounding like a horrible human being, but I owed it to her to at least try. "I'm mayor and that comes with certain expectations."

"Expectations?" Her question wasn't really a question, I knew enough about women to know that much. "Right. You're not allowed to date unless it's headed down the altar, right?" She laughed bitterly and shook her head. "I thought you were an elected official, not the Pope."

"It's not that," I answered on a sigh. "It's just that I can't be seen like I'm some sort of cad about town."

"Some sort of...," her eyes widened, and then she

laughed. "Some sort of cad about town? You didn't really just say that to me." She shook her head in anger and disbelief before her face blanked completely. "Good thing we're not dating then, isn't it?"

It was my turn to be confused. "Aren't we?"

Her shoulders fell and her expression turned sad and tired. "I haven't seen or heard from you in a week Chase, does that sound like any type of dating relationship? No," she answered her own question. "It sounds like a causal hook up, and I'm a big girl, I can handle the fact that you got what you wanted and now you're done. I just thought you were different, or at the very least that you'd have the guts to admit it."

I shook my head. "You're wrong. Dead wrong, Carlotta." I walked down the rest of the driveway until I was close enough to see that angry fluttering pulse in the base of her throat. "At first, I didn't want to seem too clingy and scare you off, and then by the third day I realized I should have reached out sooner, and it seemed, I don't know, too late to rectify. And you didn't call either, so I figured that was it." It sounded idiotic to my ears and Carlotta's grunt told me she agreed.

"You're the man Chase, and I'm an old-fashioned southern girl. I had a good time and I made sure you knew that, so you dropped the ball and I'm just responding in kind."

She was right. It was up to me to take charge, to lead

us down the path I wanted for us. "Have dinner with me. Tonight, at my place. Seven-thirty. I'll cook."

She smiled and shook her head. "I don't do pity dates."

"Good," I took another step closer and tugged on one of her wild wispy curls. "Because I don't do pity dates either. Let's call this a do-over. A proper date for a proper lady."

Carlotta rolled her eyes, but her smile told me everything I needed to know, I hadn't messed up so bad that we were over. "Fine. I'll see you at seven-thirty."

"Don't be late," I told her, pushing my luck.

She laughed and slipped inside her truck. "It's a woman prerogative to be late for any and all occasions. But I will try my best." She flashed a sweet, teasing smile and then started the engine. With a sexy finger wave, she took off and I was left there on the street, staring after her like a lovesick fool.

A quick thought occurred to me about our date tonight, and I pulled out my phone and sent a quick text.

Park in the garage. I'll leave the door open for you.

CHAPTER 17
CARLOTTA

P*ark in the garage.*

Chase's message rang inside my head like big clanging bells, warning bells, tornado alarms, all afternoon. Was I setting myself up for disappointment by agreeing to dinner? Worse, was I putting our friendship and working relationship at risk by continuing this...whatever it is we were doing?

Undoubtedly.

Did I care? Not even a little bit.

Not right now anyway. I'm sure that later, in the cold, stark light of day, I'll feel differently. But tonight, all I wanted was Chase.

However, I wanted him on my terms not his, so even though I'd slipped into my sexiest set of lingerie, lavender silk and lace, I'd covered it with jeans and a t-shirt. Completely and totally casual, just like our *rela-*

tionship. I'd made an effort, because of course I did, my mama raised a proper woman, but it wasn't the type of effort I'd make for a man with potential.

He wanted a secret relationship, a love affair on the down low, but that's not what I was about. So of course I parked my monstrous, but still ladylike truck right out front, on the street for the entire neighborhood to see.

I was nobody's secret.

I knocked on the door, and looked around the neighborhood, smiling at the sounds of families and children enjoying their evening through open windows and blinds. Chase opened the door, looking casually delicious in a pair of worn jeans and a green t-shirt that stretched across his broad chest and shoulders even as it clung to his pecs. The shirt highlighted his green eyes, making them sparkle when they took in my equally casual attire.

"Carlotta." My name came out like a breathless whisper, as if the mere sight of me was enough to steal his breath.

"Good evening, Mr. Mayor." I smiled and ignored the way my heart raced at the sight of him, but somewhere, *way* in the background those warning bells still clanged.

His lips quirked into a smile at my greeting, but a second later his brows dipped in disappointment. "You didn't park in the garage."

"Of course not. If it's a problem say so now, while there's still time for me to catch dinner elsewhere."

Tough, that was my plan going in. If he pushed it I would happily—though reluctantly—hop back in my car and head to Grady's Bar for a high calorie pastrami on rye. "Well?"

Some of that spark disappeared from his eyes, and I had a feeling that tonight wouldn't go as planned. Not how I'd planned, anyway. After a long, tense stand-off, Chase's shoulders fell in resignation, and he waved me inside.

"I'm not going to send you away Carlotta. I can't."

But he wanted to. "I'm happy to keep things casual for now Chase, but I won't be your secret or anyone else's. It's not fair to ask." I stepped inside the tidy house where nothing at all was out of place, and grinned. Chase could be so self-contained, and his home was a perfect reflection of that. "What's for dinner? It smells incredible." I turned to face him, my smile warmed up as the tension fled my body, but one look at him and it all came crashing down like a cold bucket of reality.

"I'm sorry Carlotta."

I nodded at his apology as I tried to process it, to figure out what he'd done to require an apology. "For what, exactly?"

He sighed and motioned for me to have a seat inside his living room. I chose one of two chairs that faced the sofa and crossed my legs at the ankles. "I think keeping our relationship a secret is for the best, for both of us. As mayor, the entire town will be overly invested in my relationship. They'll watch us like a hawk, report everything, every little kiss or disagreement will be bounced around for weeks. They will drop hints about getting married and having kids." He looked so distraught that I would have felt sorry for him if he hadn't been trying to keep me a secret.

I laughed at his gravely serious expression. "This is Carson Creek, Chase, the town is invested like that in every single relationship, as you well know." He'd lived here his entire life, and had been the subject of gossip a time or two. "It was only a few years ago they were all wondering if a single mayor could give the town and its problems the attention it deserved."

He knew it was true, considering his fifty year old opponent had reminded the voters of his young age and single status every chance he got.

"Which is another reason to keep this quiet."

I folded my arms and looked down my nose at Chase. This night was turning into the exact opposite of what I was hoping for when I picked out my lingerie barely an hour ago. "I wonder if it's our age difference that bothers you more than the town finding out about us."

His green eyes widened. "What? No. That's crazy." He shook his head. "I don't even think of our ages. Ever." Chase stood up and started to pace the length of the room, back and forth, back and forth while the gears cranked in his head. "Carlotta, we're not exactly low-key citizens in town," he began, but I'd had enough.

I held up a hand to stop the flow of nonsensical words from his mouth before I got really upset. "Stop it, Chase."

"Stop what?" The fact that he looked genuinely concerned and confused meant nothing to me.

"Just stop trying to explain, because you're just making things worse."

"But how can that be?"

I laughed and shook my head. "Because your words are making me mad. Look, you want something secret? Fine. I have no problem keeping a sex-only affair a secret because my sex life is no one's business but my own."

He relaxed, which told me this would likely be our last night together. "I knew you would understand."

I flashed a smile, but it was bitter and without any trace of amusement. "So, if this is just a sex-only deal there's no need for dinner. I suggest we get straight to the sex." How I managed to maintain my composure, I had no idea, but I stood and waited Chase out.

"You can't be serious."

"I can, and I am. Look Chase, I like you, but I refuse to put myself in the position of growing close to you and letting you in, when you don't even want people to know about us." I already liked him, the man he was when he could relax and be himself. I liked him more than was wise given this new development. It was time to stop thinking like a silly schoolgirl and start acting like the smart, independent woman I was.

"So that's it? It's one or the other?"

I nodded. "Yes Chase, that's how these things tend to work. Or would you rather we keep up some version of a casual relationship that has never in the history of the world worked for anyone?" I didn't need to hear his answer to know that's exactly what he was thinking.

"I just don't understand why we have to broadcast our relationship to the entire world."

I smirked. "Is that the lie you're feeding yourself? Okay fine let's say we don't *broadcast* it, but we have dinner out together once in a while. You ask me to dance at the bar and I say yes. Would that make you feel better?"

"No," he admitted reluctantly.

I got in his face. "Exactly. You want to meet up at my place or yours, romance me in secret, sleep with me and do it all in secret." My chest heaved with anger and arousal, competing emotions that shouldn't have fueled me the way they did.

Chase's green eyes darkened, and I knew he felt it too. "That's not what I'm saying at all."

"I don't care," I shot back with a bite. We were at a standoff that would end with neither of us getting what we really wanted. His gaze met mine and my own refused to waver.

I don't know who moved first, but in the next

moment our mouths were fused together in a kiss so hot I felt the flames of fire licking up the back of my neck. We kissed with as much passion as we fought, and eventually we had to pull back in search of oxygen.

Our gazes locked once again, and we attacked each other. Again. My arms wrapped around him, and I pressed up against the hard steel of his muscles, clinging to him like this was our last night together.

It is, I reminded myself. Unnecessarily, I might add.

I shoved that thought away, deep down where I wouldn't have to think of it until later. Much, much later.

Somehow my t-shirt disappeared right along with Chase's and seconds later we tumbled to the sofa. We kissed for what felt like an eternity, as if we both knew this was it, and that we needed to make the most of every second. Our tongues danced and sometimes our teeth clanked, all while our hands roamed every curve and every valley, touching and memorizing every inch of each other's body.

It was a heady experience, this kind of frantic, all-consuming feeling that coursed through my veins. I wanted him in a way I'd never wanted anyone, and I poured myself into every stroke of his hips, every nip of teeth over my sensitized skin. We came together hard and fast, and so quickly it made my head spin.

One minute my tongue flicked over his nipple and the next my body is clamped tight around his, pulsing with pleasure. "Chase." His name fell from my lips, a plea, a song, a moan and maybe even a whine. That was it.

No, *this* was it.

We were done.

Chase relaxed on top of me, and I didn't mind taking his weight, not with the plush sofa beneath my back. Breaths sawed from his lips until they eventually evened out and he pushed up to look down at me, his green eyes asking so many questions.

"We're so good together."

We were good together. Surprisingly good given the age difference and the fact that we hadn't spent any significant time together like this throughout our lives. But that's not what Chase meant. He was talking about sex. We were very sexually compatible. Highly sexually compatible compared to past lovers. But sex was the easy part. It was the part that came naturally and required little to no effort. That's what Chase meant. "Right?" His brows dipped in confusion, and then worry.

"Of course," I rushed to assure him because there was nothing wrong with the sex. It was fantastic, mind-blowing. It was exactly what sex should always be like for everyone. "It's always great between us."

"But?"

"No buts," I told him, making sure to keep my tone light and carefree. "Did I seem as if I didn't enjoy it?"

"Well no," he answered quickly and sat up, finally

rolling away from me. The cool air hit my skin, and it was exactly the dose of reality I needed, so I jumped to my feet before he could wrap me in his arms and whisper soft words in my ear.

"But something's wrong."

"Nothing is wrong Chase. I am giving you exactly what you asked for, a casual and secret encounter. My car is parked right out front and if I stay any later people will start to gossip, and I know you don't want that." Instead of facing his gaze head on, I scanned the living room in search of my jeans and wasted lavender lingerie, and I practically ran to retrieve them from a lampshade.

"Carlotta."

I closed my eyes at the anguish in his voice, against the emotions that one word made me feel. This sucked, I knew it and he did too, but this was our problem as women, we were too damn sympathetic when we didn't need to be. I refused to give in, no matter how sad or tortured he sounded, no matter how much this hurt. *It'll hurt more if you let this go on.* "Carlotta."

I spotted my sweater under the coffee table and yanked it over my head before I gathered my courage to look at Chase. "Yes?"

"Is this really it?"

I gave him a short nod. "This is what you said you wanted Chase. It's not what I want, but I'm happy to enjoy a few orgasms while I wait for Mr. Right." I stepped into my favorite black stilettos and grabbed my purse from the hook behind the front door. "I'll see you soon Chase. Good night." I opened the door and stepped out before either of us could say anything else, before Chase could use the power of his touch to reel me back inside.

No, it was better this way. Now that I knew what this was—and more importantly what it wasn't—I could adjust my expectations. And my actions.

From this moment forward there would only be two things between Chase and I, the wedding and really hot sex.

CHAPTER 18
CHASE

I'll meet you at Wheels 4 Rent at four o'clock.

Carlotta's message chimed on my phone, as straightforward and clinical as possible. For the past week that's how things were between us. Cordial, some might even say civil.

I hated it.

I absolutely fucking hated it.

What was that saying about being careful what you wish for, because you might get it? I had an unbelievably bad case of that lately. For the past week Carlotta has been nothing but cordial and professional when we met up to plan Pippa's wedding. When she came to my house—not hers, not anymore—she showed up looking beautiful, sexy enough that I couldn't wait to get her naked and beneath me, but she wasn't present. Not really. Not the way she had been before.

Before. It was such a strange word. So small, but now everything between us was split in my mind as before and after. The *after* version of Carlotta was an expert at compartmentalizing her emotions. She showed up and we had sex a few times, and she was gone before I could reach out to pull her body against mine and nibble the crook of her neck. That never failed to get her hot and bothered all over again.

It was a damn shame. I'd broken something that I hadn't realized was so special to me until it was too late. But I was determined to get it back on track.

I'll just pick you up. I texted back and held my breath.

No need. I'm already out running errands, just meet me there. That was it, there were no smiling or winking faces at the end of the message, just a period.

Busy. That was always her excuse lately. She was too busy to meet up for lunch. Too busy to talk to me on the phone. Too busy to ride together to plan Pippa and Ryan's wedding. She was a busy woman, I knew that, but I also knew it was an excuse to avoid me.

Fine. See you there.

I would have my answers today, because I needed them. Had I ruined our friendship irreparably? Would things ever be normal between us again? I was a hopeful man, no matter how determined Carlotta was to deprive me of all hope.

I arrived at Wheels 4 Rent a few minutes early,

hoping to catch Carlotta before we went inside for a quick chat, because I knew she would beat a hasty retreat the moment we were done with wedding stuff. The stubborn woman had even deprived me of that, showing up exactly at four o'clock and nodding in my direction to follow her inside.

I followed behind her and admired the fantastically feminine dress she wore. It looked like a man's dress shirt on top with short sleeves and a collar, but the floral design and the way it flared out around her knees was stunning. It was perfectly Carlotta, and I loved it.

"Carlotta Montgomery," she drawled to the guy behind the desk. "I have a four o'clock appointment with Andrew Markham."

He nodded and turned away to use the phone, and I used that moment to step in closer, to inhale her intoxicating scent. "Good afternoon, beautiful."

She gasped and took a step away from me before she turned to me. "Chase. Hello. Thank you for meeting me here." She pulled a tablet from her bag and focused on that instead of me. "I've divided the guest list into locals and out of towners, but some of the locals will also likely use the vans or mini-buses if they plan on indulging."

She was determined to be all business, and I was just as determined not to let her. "Will you be indulging?"

"Of course not," she answered without looking up. "I'll be working."

"I hope you'll have time for a dance with me?"

She shook her head again. "I will be working Chase. You should probably line up a date for the wedding if you don't want to incur Pippa's wrath."

I knew she was right, but I had no plans to indulge my sister in that way. "I'm perfectly capable of arranging my own schedule and personal life, thank you very much."

"Of course you are," she answered automatically, her gaze remained focused on that damn table until the moment Andrew Markham showed up.

"Ms. Montgomery, I'm Andrew. Come on back." His gaze slid over me, but I knew that look well, he'd already decided I was no threat to him in any way at all. "I have three mini-buses available for the dates you requested. Would you like to take a look at them?"

Carlotta nodded and I kept my distance, watching as Andrew tried his best to charm her while talking leather interior and air conditioning. Somehow the man actually pulled it off and she was all smiles and sweet giggles for him. But me, one of her oldest friends? I got worse than the silent treatment, I got no treatment at all aside from a few questions about Pippa's preferences.

Thirty minutes later the buses were booked for the weekend, with drivers, and Carlotta rushed from the building as if she was being chased.

"Carlotta, wait up!" Her steps never slowed, but

luckily I had a height advantage and easily closed the gap between us. "Are you just going to avoid me for the rest of our lives?"

She sighed and stopped, her gaze blank as it fixed on my face. "I'm not avoiding you, Chase."

"No, then what in the hell are you doing?" My tone was harsh, but dammit this was ridiculous.

She folded her arms, her demeanor a picture of defiance. "What I'm doing is trying to plan a wedding and half a dozen other events, Chase. What are *you* doing?"

"I'm just trying to get some answers."

"No. You regret that things are different between us even though you wanted them to be different. This is your doing, not mine, so please don't try to rewrite history." She shook her head and let out an unamused grunt. "I don't know if this is misplaced guilt or morning after regrets, but I'm a big girl Chase. I don't need you to check on me. I'm fine."

"I'm glad one of us is," I huffed. "Because I'm so far from fine that I can hardly think straight."

"I'm sorry about that Chase, but we're adults and we must live with the consequences of our actions."

"So, this is punishment?"

She let out a laugh that lacked any trace of humor. "How am I punishing you, when you get the secrecy you apparently crave without giving up the sex? If anything, you're coming out ahead in this little agreement." She shook her head and stepped up into her giant truck. "This will get easier Chase."

"Yeah, when?" I asked with a growl.

She shrugged and turned over the engine. "Eventually."

That's exactly what I was afraid of.

CHAPTER 19
CARLOTTA

When my doorbell rang at six o'clock, my breath hitched. It was unlikely that I would find Chase on the other side of that door given our last conversation, but I couldn't prevent my stupid heart from hoping. I slowly exhaled and opened the door.

"Pippa, this is a nice surprise. What are you and Ryanna doing here?"

Pippa rolled her eyes and pressed a kiss to Ryanna's head before handing the baby to me. "I need some big girl conversation. And lots of food that I shouldn't be eating."

"You've come to the right place," I assured her and stepped back so she could drag the baby's stroller and diaper bag inside. Ryanna was wide awake with a sweet smile on her face as I bounced her. "She's grown so much in just a few weeks."

"Right? I'm worried that I'll wake up tomorrow and she'll be a surly teenager." Pippa laughed and reached for her daughter, laughing even harder when I pulled back. "Hey, no fair."

"Consider this me giving you a small break that you didn't ask for."

"Thanks," she said on a sigh and dropped down on the sofa. She tucked her legs under herself and settled into a comfortable position. "First, let's order food, and then you can tell me how the wedding planning is coming along?"

We took a quick break to browse menus before we settled on pizza with garlic bread and wings. And cookies. Lots and lots of cookies. We settled on the sofa again with iced tea at our sides and Ryanna still in my arms.

"Wedding plans are going well." I updated her on all the details. "Next up is invitations and flowers, if you have any ideas."

Pippa nodded, and her thoughtful expression told me she had given it some thought. "I was thinking white flowers, all types as long as they're white, accented with some yellow flowers, and maybe silver ribbons on the vases and bouquets?"

I beamed a smile at her. "Those are details I can work with. Thanks." I leaned over and grabbed the closest notepad to jot down her ideas.

"You're welcome," she shot back quickly. "Now, what's going on between you and my brother?"

I don't know if it was her words or her tone that put me on edge, but I risked a look at Pippa who seemed more amused than anything. Still, I couldn't give in that easily. "He's helping me plan your wedding just as you requested."

"I'm calling a big fat BS on that. There's something going on, and your denial only tells me that it's more than spending time together." Her blue eyes stared a hole into me, and I felt my resolve start to crumble. "Spill. Now."

"There's nothing to spill," I assured her. "There was a moment, a brief one, where I thought or maybe *we* thought it could be something more. But as it turns out, we were both wrong." That was the most expedient answer that didn't force me to think too hard about how much I missed Chase, and how easy and fun things were between us.

Pippa shook her head and dropped her face in her hands with a groan. "My brother is the world's biggest idiot."

"He's not. He and I just want, or rather, expect, different things. So we decided to shelve anything personal and keep it professional. And platonic." Except for the regular orgasms we still shared.

"Is that why he was so miserable when he came by for dinner yesterday?" My eyes widened in shock, and

Pippa laughed. "That's what I thought. He had that hang-dog expression he used to have when he got a B in school. He was grumpy and pouting, but refused to talk about it."

I shrugged off her words and evaded her knowing looks. "It's probably work."

"It's not. He was confused and grouchy, and Chase is always sure and confident when it comes to work."

"He's confident and sure about a lot of things." Including wanting to keep a real relationship secret. "Anyway, there's nothing to tell, unless you have a burning desire to hear details of your brother's sex life."

Pippa's eyelids slammed shut and she smacked her hands over her ears. "Ew. Yuck. No thank you, please." After her dramatics were over, Pippa sighed. "This is going to end badly for both of you, please tell me you know that?"

"It won't, in fact. I have it all under control, I promise."

Pippa slid to the edge of her seat and rested her chin on her hands. "This I've got to hear."

"Simple. We plan the wedding together and we sleep together, but that's it. We don't hang out or cuddle or share meals anymore. There's a line in the sand that I won't allow us to cross."

Her brows dipped in confusion. "To make sure you don't fall for him?"

I nodded because there was no point in lying. "To safeguard us both from confusion and hurt feelings."

"No wonder he's so miserable."

"He got exactly what he wanted, so there's no reason for anyone to be miserable." Least of all him.

"No. My brother is a man built for a relationship. He's too literal and too straightforward to succeed at something as complicated as friends with benefits."

"Well, I don't *do* secret relationships. I do, however, do secret sex liaisons." I ignored the voice in my head that said if Chase was built for relationships, then maybe he just didn't want one with me. "It's fine Pippa. You don't need to worry about this. Your brother and I are both adults and we know what we're doing. And if one of us ends up hurt, that pain will heal."

Her assessing gaze remained fixed on me for a long time, but instead of squirming under her scrutiny, I turned my attention to the adorable bundle of pink in my arms. She was small, soft and smelled so good, and only one thought ran through my mind.

I want this.

I wanted it desperately, and the more time I wasted with Chase, no matter how great that time was, the more I cheated myself out of a chance to have a baby, a family of my own someday.

"This won't impact my wedding?"

"Nope. I am a total professional, and I am offended you even have to ask."

Pippa's shoulders fell. "I just want to be sure."

"If you're so worried about it, tell Chase he's off the hook. I have what I need to finalize the last few details on my own."

She shook her head. "If I do that, he'll think I'm punishing him or taking your side over his."

"There are no sides here, Pip. We just want different things. That's all." She stared at me, and I stared at her, neither of us willing to break the hold as if it was some kind of contest. A battle of wills that only ended when the doorbell rang. "Food," I said and jumped up, accidentally jostling Ryanna.

"I'll get it," Pippa insisted and stood with a pointed glare for me. "While I do that, I want you to think about what you would tell me in this exact same situation."

Pippa walked off and left me along with thoughts that wouldn't stop, no matter how hard I tried to shut them down.

CHAPTER 20
CHASE

My thoughts were all over the place, an unusual feeling for me, as I tried to focus on a proposal for a town hall makeover. A makeover, like this historic building was an overtired new mother instead of a piece of Carson Creek history. Did people really talk like that, using words like makeover for a building? I didn't have the answer yet, even though I'd spent the past ten minutes thinking about the semantics rather than the proposal itself.

And this was all because of a woman who had scrambled my brain and my ability to think clearly.

"He's not available right now, but I will be happy to pass along a message if you care to leave one." CJ's voice filtered through my muddled thoughts and I frowned. She was using that tone I told her I didn't like, where she sounded like some hostess at a trendy restaurant, wielding what little power she had as my gatekeeper.

Except I didn't play that game, not with anyone. If I had time, I indulged any citizen or interested business with a conversation. I wondered who had earned that tone, since I hadn't heard the phone ring or the office door open and shut.

"No thanks," Carlotta's voice reached me, her tone almost amused. "I'll just give him a call."

"I said he's unavailable," CJ said with a bite to her words.

"Oh, I heard you honey," she drawled in a sickly sweet tone. "And I told you that I will call Chase directly. You have a good day."

She's leaving.

I was out of my chair in a flash, pausing only briefly so I wouldn't look as desperate to set eyes on Carlotta as I felt. *Ready.* I smoothed the fabric on the chest of my blazer and released a relaxing breath.

"Carlotta, this is a surprise. What brings you by?"

She smiled a little too brightly, but I didn't imagine the heat in her eyes as she held up a stack of cards. "Invitation samples. You have time?"

"For you? Always." I smiled and motioned her inside my office, stopping for a moment to glare at CJ. "We need to have a chat. Later," I told her and closed my door, a clear indicator that *now* I did not want to be disturbed.

I turned towards Carlotta and sighed. She was here, and she'd come on her own. Sure, it was to look at wedding invitations, but she was here. "So, wedding invitations?"

She nodded, and when I sat behind my desk, a dazzling smile greeted me. "Yes." She laid out a dozen cards, all of them different in subtle ways. The fonts and the colors of the words, the color of the paper, even the weight of the paper. They were all just different enough. "Wedding invitations."

I looked again and frowned. "Why didn't you consult me on this?" Realizing how heavy handed that sounded, I leaned back in my chair with a sigh. "I didn't mean it like that, it's just, are you avoiding me?"

"Nope. Pippa dropped by unexpectedly a few days ago, she gave me all the details I needed. It was completely incidental Chase, I promise."

I didn't like the answer, because it didn't feel like the whole truth, but I nodded, accepting her words at face value. "All right. How have you been?" I hadn't seen her in a few days.

She smiled softly, it was the kind of smile you live for days on without food or water. "Good. Busy as usual, but good. You?"

"Distracted," I shot back quickly.

"Chase," she began, her tone apologetic, but I didn't want an apology or sympathy.

"Tell me," I rushed in quickly, interrupting her.

"How am I supposed to pick one invitation when they're all identical?"

She laughed as I hoped she would, the melodic sound removing much of the tension from the room. "Not quite identical," she grinned. "Just look at each of them carefully, and tell me which ones call out to you, or which you find most pleasing to the eye."

"You're pretty pleasing to the eye," I told her honestly. She'd shown up in a sexy butter colored dress that emphasized the summer sun that had kissed her chest and shoulders, bouncy brown waves and red lips. She was gorgeous. "Can we just put this picture of you on the invitations?"

"For your sister's wedding? That would hardly be appropriate." Her tone was admonishing, but her smile gave away the truth.

"That's okay. Pip's always been a little inappropriate."

She laughed outright at that. "I'll be sure to tell her you said so."

"She knows the truth," I shot back as my smile grew even wider as we stared at each other for a long time. Then my smile dimmed. "I miss you Carlotta."

"I'm here now Chase, and we saw each other just a few days ago." Her tone came out gentle, but I could see the longing in her eyes. She missed me too.

I shook my head. "That was for sex. I miss hearing your

voice and talking to you." Who knew that losing her from my life would feel like a lost limb? We'd been friends for most of our lives, but not how we were friends now, and losing that as swiftly as I did, felt like I'd lost my best friend.

"Well you can hear my voice tonight when we take more photos of the barn."

That wasn't enough. "Have dinner with me after? We'll go wherever you want." I needed to spend time with her again. Maybe our connection wasn't as powerful as I imagined, maybe it really was just lust, and another date would prove that.

Carlotta's expression shifted to surprise, her perfect brows dipped in confusion. "Why?"

"Because Carlotta, I miss talking to you and hearing your take on things. I miss the sound of that sexy drawl of yours. I miss you, period and I want that back." That admission was difficult but it was the truth. "I just miss you Car."

Her lips tugged into a reluctant grin at the nickname. "I miss you too Chase, but this is for the best. For both of us."

"I don't think so." Missing her like this was untenable, unsustainable for me. I couldn't miss her like I did and be the mayor the town elected me to be. "If being in public is what it takes to have you back in my life, fully and completely, that's what I'm willing to do." It felt so good to get the words out, difficult as they were, but they were out there now and things could go back to normal.

Or so I thought.

Carlotta's expression shifted, and she shook her head, refusing rather than accepting my compromise. "I don't want you to do anything you don't want to do Chase, such as appearing in public with me and giving people the exact right impression of why we're spending time together."

"This is the compromise I thought you wanted." Now I was just confused as hell.

"No, this isn't a compromise Chase. This is a sacrifice you're willing to make just to get what you want. Me. You'll hate it, and maybe even resent me eventually, so no, I think we should keep going as we have been."

I huffed my anger and my disgust. "You mean just showing up at each other's houses for sex and leaving without any laughs or conversation, or even a fucking meal?" She winced at my curse, but I didn't bat an eyelash because I meant what I said.

"We can always end our sexual relationship if it's no longer giving you what you need." Her stiff and formal tone stung. "I miss you too Chase, a lot more than I can possibly tell you, but indulging in something we don't both want simply because it'll feel good in the moment..." She stared down at the invitations for a long moment and I wondered if she had more to say, but she just blinked, stood up and walked out of my office.

"Dammit," I growled in frustration. Why couldn't she see that I was trying? That I wanted her more than I'd wanted a woman in a long time, and I was willing to compromise so that we both got what we wanted.

But her words, her accusations rang in my head for the rest of the day. Was I simply sacrificing just so I could spend time with her? Would that, as she said, only make the pain worse in the end? Could the pain possibly be any worse than it was now?

I had more questions than answers by the time I left the office for the day, and my mind wouldn't stop chewing it over. Was our relationship already over and I just hadn't accepted it yet? Was it inevitable, or was it, as Pippa had accused, my focus on keeping my private life invisible that doomed us?

It was that word, invisible, that had gotten to me. It was why I wanted to give going public a shot. I wasn't looking for a relationship invisible from the public eye, but I did want a few parts of my life that were just for me.

Was that so wrong?

CHAPTER 21
CARLOTTA

"I think that's enough photos. What do you think?" I arrived at the barn fifteen minutes early to make sure I didn't have to spend too much time with Chase. After today's conversation I knew it was best that we maintained a healthy and professional distance from one another. "Well?" I folded my arms and waited for him to respond.

Chase rubbed his jaw, like he was deep in thought when I knew he didn't care, not about the photos or how the barn would ultimately look for the wedding reception. "Does this roof need to be, I don't know, sanded or something? It looks a little rough."

I smiled at his attempt to offer some feedback. "It's rustic."

"Then yes, I think there are plenty of photos." His gaze settled on me for so long I felt a little unnerved, and more than a little certain that he was working his way up to another talk.

"Great." I gave the barn one final look with a critical eye and turned towards the door. If I walked fast enough, sidestepping the debris in the middle of the barn, I could make it out of here and to my car before Chase got out whatever he was trying to say.

"Carlotta." My name exited his mouth in a defeated tone that touched me in a way I hadn't anticipated. "Please."

My shoulders fell forward, because I knew there was no way to get out of this talk. "Don't do this Chase. Please."

"Don't do what? All I'm trying to do is spend time with you Carlotta. Is that so wrong?"

"It's not wrong, no." I turned to him against my better judgment, because I knew the anguish in his green eyes would get to me. His broad shoulders were hunched in defeat. "But to what end?"

His brows dipped in confusion. "To the end that we get to spend more time together."

"You are purposely misunderstanding me Chase."

"I'm not. I said I was willing to go on a date, in public, and you shot that idea down, so I really don't know what else you want from me."

"What I want is for you to *want* to go on a date with me. Out in public where people in this town may or may not see us. I don't want you to be *willing* to go on a date."

I wanted to believe that this was just a poorly misworded proposition, but I couldn't believe him. I didn't.

"I want to spend time with you Carlotta. However I can."

"But you would prefer that we spend time together in your house or mine." It wasn't a question. "That's exactly what we're doing now."

"No. We're meeting up to have sex. That's it." His nostrils flared, and I stood a little taller, arms folded so I could stare right back at him.

"And that's a problem, how exactly?"

"Dammit Carlotta, I want more than that!"

I nodded because after talking with Pippa I understood, but figuring out his life for him wasn't my job. "I get that, but what you want and what I want don't match up. You want a secret relationship, where we spend our free time together and no one knows about it. I got that loud and clear Chase. But what about what I want? To go out on dates and have long weekends. Family holidays. I want someone who is free to go after everything, the whole picture. And I want it done out in the open." He couldn't possibly be this callous, could he?

"And we can't do that?" He seemed genuinely confused, and that only stirred my anger, made it hotter and bigger and more furious.

I let my arms drop to my side, but that didn't feel right and I slid them up to my hips. "Chase, I can't spend all of my time with a man who clearly isn't ready for a relationship, and I won't waste my time and miss my chance to find real love."

He took a step back as if I'd struck him. "So time with me is wasted if it doesn't lead to marriage?"

"No, if it has no possibility of being anything more than a dirty little secret, *then* it's a waste of time."

His nostrils flared again as he took in a deep breath and let it out so slowly a full minute passed before he spoke. "I told you we could go out on a date, but you said no. Now I'm starting to think you never wanted anything more than a friends with benefits arrangement."

"Then you should be happy that whatever this was, it's over now." It broke my heart to say those words, to say them right to his face, but it had to be done. "Good night, Chase." I turned on my heels once again, and this time I made it to the entrance of the barn before I felt his hand on my shoulder.

"Wait, please. I'm sorry." He sighed a few times as if he was trying to figure out what he wanted to say, but couldn't find the right words. I refused to look at him, because I knew what I'd see on his face, what I felt in my heart. Regret.

"There's no point waiting or being sorry Chase. We're good together, I know it and you do too, but I am falling for you, and I won't do that while you keep us a secret from the world." There, those were the words that would in all likelihood send him running.

"You're what?"

"You heard me," I said back. "I'm not going to sugarcoat things with you Chase. I like you, a lot, but that's irrelevant because I will never, ever again let a man make me feel like I'm not good enough."

"That's not what I'm doing," he insisted, his gaze seared me. "I swear."

"Maybe not intentionally, but the result is the same isn't it?" We stood there for a long moment, two immovable objects waiting for the other to break, to crack.

He groaned low in his throat, and a hot second later Chase pulled me closer and pressed his body flush against mine. He smiled slowly as he leaned in, and it only disappeared when his lips were on mine. A fire sparked deep in my core.

My belly clenched hard, and I thought about fighting it. I seriously considered pushing him away in the name of self-preservation. I didn't though, because I couldn't. This was Chase, and I wanted him, any part of him, and in this moment I wanted all of him.

So I wrapped my arms around him and pressed against him so he knew that whatever this was, whatever it was meant to be, right now I was all in.

He kissed me and I kissed him, and we stood there half inside the barn and half under the moonlight. His grip tightened around me and I moaned into his mouth, tilting back to let him deepen the intoxicating kiss. My head was dizzy and my heart raced while Chase used his mouth and hands to drive me wild. Big manly hands sculpted my curves, almost worshipped them, and it made me feel beautiful and desired, sexy as hell.

He pulled back first with a low growl, a heartbeat before his mouth went to my neck, heating tiny fires all over my shoulders and neck and chest before he nibbled my jaw. "Carlotta. I need you."

I closed my eyes and said the only thing I could. "Yes." I wanted him too, and now was not the time to deny it, not when I was close to having it all. For tonight, anyway.

Chase dropped to his knees and looked up at me with an affectionate smile that caused my heart to skip a beat. "I miss you, Car."

I miss you too.

I thought the words, but I didn't say them. I couldn't. Not when things were so mixed up between us, not when tonight could only be for tonight. My eyes fluttered shut at the feel of his day old scruff against my thighs, and the sound of him breathing in my intimate scent made me pulse. The cool night air touched the bare, slick skin between my thighs and I gasped.

And then his mouth, hot and damp, was on my most sensitive spot. He ravished me like I was his favorite meal, kissed me and licked at my flesh until one hand clenched his hair and the other grasped at the barn wall. "Chase," I gasped and my hips rolled in time to the swipe of his tongue.

He groaned against me and lifted one leg over his shoulder and then he absolutely devoured me. He gave me all the pleasure my body could stand, and then a little bit more until my guttural, animalistic sounds bounced off the barn walls. He flicked his hot heavy tongue over my clit and my hips bucked, hungry for more of his magical mouth.

The sound of his erotic growls tore my eyes open and I stared up at the moon, so big and bright in the dark starless night, like it was lit just for me, just for this moment right here. "Yes, Chase." My words were breathless and choppy, I grasped his hair with both hands as my head thrashed back and forth against the barn wall, and then in one long moment, pleasure fell over me like a giant wave, pulling me under and tossing me about until I thought I might drown in the sensations he produced within me.

And then I was falling, though it felt more like floating, like a piece of paper floating on a gentle breeze with the pitch black sky and the oversized moon directly above it. It was a special form of heaven and it was just for me.

For us.

Chase stood and spun me around, leaving me no choice but to plant my hands on the wall of the barn as he tilted my hips and tore my panties down, the act pulled a gasp from me. "You taste divine," he whispered in my ear, his voice harsh as he tugged down his zipper, the sound of his belt buckle jangling tightened my core again.

And then he was right where he was meant to be, buried deep inside me. He froze and let out a long sigh that sounded like relief or something similar. His hips started to pump furiously, as though he was afraid I might change my mind, might decide that my body didn't need his particular brand of ecstasy.

That was of course, crazy, because not even wild dogs could have pulled us apart at that moment, with his hips pistoning in and out like a high performance machine. He was hard and long and thick, and he was the one thing my body craved above all else.

My hips tilted even more and he slipped deeper, drawing a shocked gasp from both of us. The pleasure was overwhelming, and I closed my eyes and allowed myself to enjoy this for what it was, two bodies desperate for something else they couldn't have, but settling for carnal pleasure.

"Carlotta," he growled and nipped my earlobe.

"Yes," I whispered back, afraid any sounds might ruin the magic woven around us.

Those were the last words either of us spoke as our collective pleasure built and we climbed that hill of pleasure, breathlessly, together. He panted and growled, I cried out and moaned, and then we were both shouting our pleasure into the moonlight. For several long moments we stayed there, panting hard and gasping, willing our bodies to prolong the pleasure.

But all good things must come to an end, as they say. And this? It was, without a doubt, our ending.

"Go out with me, Car." His command was punctuated by a gentle kiss that started at my shoulder and moved up my neck. "Please."

It was that growled plea that got to me, that and orgasmic high I was still on. Maybe it was just the fact that I was already half in love with this man, but the word fell from my lips before I could stop it.

"Yes."

I said yes because I missed him, because I wanted more time with him. I said yes because could things, really and truly, get any worse?

CHAPTER 22
CHASE

"You look beautiful."

My breath caught in my chest at the sight of her as she opened the door in a gorgeous, wine colored dress that deepened the brown in her eyes and hair. She was a dream come true, and I was thrilled she'd finally given in and said yes.

"Thank you Chase. You look good too." Her gaze slid up and down my frame before they flared with heat. She blinked, and that heat was gone. "Let me just grab my purse." She shut the door, disappeared and reappeared within a minute. "Okay. Where are we going?" Carlotta locked the door and strode beside me, giving off no vibes that this was an actual date.

"That is a surprise." I'd spent the past twenty-four hours searching for the perfect place in Carson Creek to make our debut—sort of—as a couple. "How was your day?"

She shrugged, but maintained a serene smile as we stopped at the passenger side of my car. "Good. Busy as usual, but I made a lot of progress on several different projects. How was yours?"

"Busy and boring," I told her with a laugh. "But the excitement of my job is in the details." I smiled from the driver's side and she returned the smile, though it wasn't her usual megawatt smile, the one that made me feel like the best man on Earth. Like the man who'd earned that smile from her.

"As long as it makes you happy," she said, her tone upbeat, but it still felt off, as if she were here but not really.

The drive to the restaurant was friendly enough, filled with small talk which got the evening off to a pretty good start, at least I thought so. I opened Carlotta's door and helped her from the passenger seat, smiling as she shivered when my hand on her lower back sent my thumb in contact with her bare skin.

I felt her smile before I saw it when we came to a stop outside Franco's Trattoria. It was a small Italian restaurant with daily specials and fresh pasta. "Franco's? This isn't exactly a lowkey venue Chase."

I stood a little taller and my gaze met hers. "I know. I wanted you to know that I'm serious about this."

Satisfied with my answer, her smile softened and her

shoulders relaxed. "All right then, let's do this shall we?"

I kept my hand at her lower back and guided her inside. "Mayor Carson, it's nice to see you out tonight. Your table is right this way." The young hostess wore a bright smile as she took in the woman beside me. "Carlotta, that is an incredible dress."

"Thank you." She flashed a bright beauty queen smile. "I should have had you do my hair though, that is a work of art."

The hostess blushed and then turned to lead us to our table. Franco's wasn't full, and I allowed myself to relax. Maybe tonight wouldn't be so bad after all. "Your server will be here soon. Our specials are right in front. Enjoy your meal."

When we were alone, Carlotta smiled. "They've made some changes since I was last here." She looked around the dimly lit dining room, examining all the changes. "I'm glad they changed out the white tablecloths, it's so old school."

"You've been here a lot?"

She nodded. "Here and there. It's a good place for a date, and they have the best pappardelle I've ever had." She leaned in with a conspiratorial smile. "Don't tell Nina."

"Your secret is safe with me," I deadpanned.

Carlotta laughed and turned her focus to the menu, giving me time to just observe her. She was a woman who did everything full-on, whether it was planning an event or simply offering up a compliment. Her super power was making everyone feel better, as if they had her full attention at any given moment. Her brown eyes lit up as she browsed the menu and licked her lips. "Everything sounds so delicious, or maybe I'm just outrageously hungry," she laughed again and shook her head. "What looks good to you?"

"You," I said simply, and watched as heat flared in her eyes turning them to molten lava.

"Good answer, but I'm not on the menu right now."

"But later?" I asked hopefully.

"Maybe," she said coyly just as our server arrived, a twentysomething kid named Dave who was helping Trey with his social media business.

"Hey lovebirds, what can I get you to drink this evening?" The kid didn't notice my wince and kept on with his spiel on wine and cocktail specials. "There's a nice rose Moscato that goes perfectly with spicy sausage sauce, and surprisingly, it goes well with the house vodka sauce too."

"Really? Wine and vodka?" Carlotta gave the boy her full attention. "You've piqued my curiosity Dave."

He smiled back. "I'm happy to bring a sample glass if you're not sure?"

"That would be great, thank you." When Dave was gone she turned back to me with a frown. "What's wrong?"

"What do you mean? Nothing's wrong."

She sighed, her body sagged with disappointment, leaving me to wonder what I'd done wrong. "You were frowning at Dave like he spit in your food."

"Was I?" All of her attention had been on him, so how in the hell had she noticed?

"Never mind." She turned her attention back to the menu until Dave returned with the sample, which she loved. "I'll have a nice, big glass of that Dave. Thank you."

He returned a few minutes later with our drinks and a massive Italian charcuterie board. "From Franco, for the happy couple." He said the words with a wide smile before he turned and walked away.

The happy couple, he said as if our relationship status was any of his business. "Why would he say that?"

Carlotta's brows dipped in confusion. "What does it matter? If you care that much, correct him when he returns. Or better yet, send the board back and ask for the 'just friends' board."

My shoulders fell, I was screwing this up. Big time. "I'm sorry. Let's enjoy it."

She grabbed a slice of prosciutto wrapped around a cheese stuffed chili pepper and groaned. "It really does pair well with this. Want to taste?"

"No," I barked, suddenly uncomfortable with the intimacy she was proposing. I looked around, and sure enough, several sets of eyeballs were focused on us. Too focused.

"Right." Her voice was void of emotion, but she looked as cool and as calm as could be, tasting the elements of the board and sipping her wine as if she were out to dinner alone. "So good," she whispered to herself and tried another cheese and pepper combination.

With nothing else to say for the moment, I picked up a slice of spicy salami and folded a piece of mozzarella around it, tasting it with a groan of satisfaction. "It is delicious." The table was tense and I hated it, worse I had no clue how to get us back on track. "I'm sorry Car."

She blinked and looked up at me as if only now noticing I was still there. "Whatever for?"

"This isn't going how I planned." Looking at the situation now, I don't even know how I expected the evening to go. She said nothing, but her head tilted and she gave me a strange look as if I was some kind of puzzle to figure out. It made me feel uncomfortable, so I searched for another topic. "Are you going to Summer Movies in the Park?" Every summer the town put on movies in the park to encourage family time and to take make sure our older citizens got out of the house and socialized.

"Probably. I try to go a few times each summer if my schedule allows it."

It was on the tip of my tongue to ask her if she wanted to go with me, another date, but much more lowkey than tonight had been already. But just as I opened my mouth to pose the question, a shadow fell over the table.

Carlotta looked up with a surprised smile for the former mayor of Carson Creek, Herb Riley and his wife Eleanor. "Mayor Riley, this is a nice surprise. What are you all doing here?" She stood and hugged the older couple.

"Date night," Mrs. Riley said proudly. "Now that he's not so busy running the town, Herb is determined to romance me all over again."

I resisted the urge to roll my eyes as Carlotta sucked in a breath. "Well that is just fantastic, and the sweetest thing. Good for you both."

"Thank you, sweetie." Mrs. Riley's gaze fell to me. "And it's good to see the current mayor making an effort at work-life balance. We were all afraid you'd remain single until your terms were over," she said with a laugh.

Mayor Riley let out a bark of laughter. "Carlotta is exactly the kind of wife you need if you want to move up the political ladder, son. Exactly perfect, just like my Eleanor here."

One finger slid between my skin and my shirt collar at his words and I tried for a tight smile. "Uh, thanks."

Carlotta laughed. "Chase and I are just renewing an old friendship," she offered as an explanation.

Eleanor laughed. "That's how Herb and I got together too," she said with a suggestive lilt to her voice.

I had to bite back a groan, and thankfully, the

hostess showed up to take them to their table on the other side of the restaurant

Thank goodness.

"Thanks for that," I said to Carlotta with a weak smile.

She didn't smile back, and she didn't reply, she just reached for her glass and finished it off before flagging down Dave for another.

By the time our entrees arrived, two more people had stopped at our table to tell me what a good job I'd done, choosing to romance Carlotta. It was damned exhausting, and why was the whole damn town so focused on my love life? "How's your dinner," I asked an unusually quiet Carlotta.

She shrugged. "It's delicious," she answered and turned back to her food.

"Mine too," I said even though she hadn't asked.

Alice and Mabel Turner stopped at the table just as we finished our entrees. "Mr. Mayor, it's such a delight to see you doing something other than work," Alice cooed.

"Indeed," Mabel added with a wide smile. "It's darn good to see you dating, Chase. A man like you should be married with children, and Carlotta will make a mighty fine wife."

Was it getting hotter in the restaurant? My pulse raced and my heart slammed against my chest at the expectations. They were ruining my ability to relax and to enjoy this first date with her, dammit. "Um, sure. Thanks."

When they were gone Carlotta glared at me. "Their words are just their own opinions, Chase. No one is proposing a shotgun wedding, or any other kind."

I nodded and reached for my water, guzzling down the whole thing before I reached for her untouched glass. "Yes, I know."

"Do you? Because you're acting as if you don't know."

Franco the Third chose that moment to make his appearance at our table. He was a loud and boisterous man with thick black hair and a patch of gray at each temple. Unlike his father and grandfather, he didn't sport the pot belly, or the thick black moustache. "I have made a wonderfully delicious and romantic dessert for the happy couple!" His words were so loud I cringed as I risked a glance around the restaurant.

All eyes were on us.

"It smells divine," Carlotta responded easily. "Is that amaretto I smell?"

"Good nose," he said flirtatiously. "Only the finest for you. Go on, taste it."

I couldn't move, could only watch as Carlotta dipped her spoon into the spongy cake until she made her way to the thick, chocolatey center. As soon as the chocolate touched her tongue, she let out a low sensual moan and lust slammed against me with the force of an eighteen wheeler.

"Oh wow Franco, that is magnificent."

He laughed, fully pleased with her praise. "Feed some to your fella, let's see how our mayor likes it."

I held up a hand with a tight smile. "That won't be necessary. I'm capable of feeding myself." To that end, I grabbed a spoon and took a bite, surprised at how delicious it was. "Incredible," I sighed and offered the chef a smile.

"Perfect! Enjoy," he commanded and walked off, leaving our table in yet another tense silence.

The evening hadn't gone to plan at all. I tried, I really had. This night was meant to show Carlotta that I could do this, that I could handle a public relationship, but it had only proven the opposite. Everyone digging into my personal life, offering up opinions on my choice of woman, assuming we were destined for marriage and babies. It was too much pressure, too presumptuous, and I hated every damn moment of it.

I chanced a look at Carlotta, at first glance she seemed totally unbothered by it all, but as I looked closer I could see the tight lines pinched around her mouth, the ramrod straight set of her spine, the lines of strain around her eyes. She looked uncomfortable, or maybe furious.

"This didn't go as planned," I offered with a smile of commiseration.

She didn't smile back. "You know what I think Chase? I think this evening went just as you planned."

"What? How could you-,"

She took her time responding, taking two more bites of the lava cake before she pushed it away, seemingly disgusted. She reached for her glass of wine and finished it off too. "You brought me to one of the busiest restaurants in town, in the middle of town, where you knew there would be no peace. You did it on purpose, but what I can't figure out is why. Were you hoping this would convince me that you were right and we should keep us a secret?"

Had I? Were my motives so cold and calculating.

She laughed. "You don't even know, do you?" She laughed again, bitterly this time, and she dabbed the corners of her mouth and dropped the napkin on the table. "Yeah well thanks Chase for *trying*."

"I did try," I insisted with a fire I didn't truly feel.

"You keep telling yourself that Chase. I hope it makes you feel better about things." She stood and fixed a smile on her face before she leaned forward to whisper in my ear. "Now you can stop trying, because I'm done. Thanks for dinner." She walked away and with my back facing the door, I couldn't risk letting my gaze follow her without drawing more stares. More gossip.

I finished off the lava cake, paid the bill and made my way home knowing that Carlotta and I were a thing of the past.

CHAPTER 23
CARLOTTA

"Is it weird how excited I am about being here for Movies in the Park?" Pippa's blue eyes were bright, and so excited they were almost shiny. "Getting out of the house and putting on a nice dress feels good, and I haven't been to one of these in forever."

I looked up at her from my spot on the blanket covering the grass and smiled. "Well you look great. Peach is definitely your color." Sexy waves brushed against her shoulders where a few freckles appeared. "I don't usually get to attend because this is prime wedding weather. I guess I just got lucky this year.

"Thanks. Can you tell Ryanna and I have been spending a lot of time in the backyard?"

I nodded. "The tan is a dead giveaway, unless you've been on a tropical vacation without me."

She rolled her eyes and placed Ryanna in my arms. "I wish."

"I love her outfit, her eyes look an unreal shade of blue with this denim jumper."

"Right? So adorable." Pippa settled herself and two big bags on the blanket with a sigh. "Let's get a photo of Aunt Carlotta and Ryanna." She snapped a few photos of us, smiling at each one before snapping another.

Holding the baby in my arms was just what I needed. She was so tiny and so soft, her baby babble soothed my frazzled nerves. After my disastrous final date with Chase, I needed something to relax me and distract me from thinking about it.

"What's in the basket," Pippa asked, a smile in her tone.

Her question pulled me from my wayward thoughts, thoughts that I'd promised myself I was done thinking about. "Look and find out." I spent the morning putting together a picnic basket for us to enjoy today. It was another distraction to keep my mind off Chase and that ridiculous attempt at a date.

Pippa squealed as she peeked inside the picnic basket. "You made bacon wrapped dates? Oh my god, and prosciutto wrapped melon? You are a goddess," she enthused.

I couldn't help but smile at her excitement. "I figured you were in need of grown up talk and grown up food for your big day out."

"I really appreciate it," she said as she laid out the picnic items. "I'll be excited when Ryan is back home. I love my sweet baby girl, but I could use a day off."

I laughed. "Anyone in town would be happy to babysit," I told her. "If only some stubborn mama would ask."

"I know, but I'd miss her or feel like a bad mom, or something. I've been taking her with me to the restaurant because it hurts to be without her." She bit her bottom lip and then let out a nervous huff of laughter. "Enough about me and my issues, tell me about you. What's going on?"

"Not much really, just busy working. There is always a wedding or party to plan." Business was good, which was crucial when you worked for yourself.

"That's good, really. Awesome. But you know that's not what I'm talking about."

I nodded because I did know what she was getting at, but I didn't want to talk about it, even if I knew there was no getting out of this conversation.

"So," her blue eyes were wide with an expectant look on her face. "Tell me about your date. It's all anyone in town can talk about."

Which only served to prove Chase's point. "It was a disaster," I told her bluntly.

"What? No! How can that be?"

I sucked in a deep breath and took in Ryanna's serene expression as she stared up at the blue sky and the clouds passing by, letting it out slowly as I wished for an ounce of her serenity. "It was just a show Pip."

Her brows dipped in confusion, because while she knew her brother well, she did not know him as a man. As a brother, and a mayor sure, but not the man I saw at dinner a few nights ago.

"Explain please."

I did exactly that. I told her all about curious residents who stopped by our table to say perfectly nice things about him or me, or both of us. "With every person who stopped by, his expression grew tense. Words of surprise or excitement or encouragement only made it worse. By the time we finished our meal, his lips were pulled into a tight white line and he was totally stressed out."

She nodded knowingly, but her eyes held nothing but sympathy. "So how was it just a show?"

I recounted our previous argument. "He did this as a concession according to him, but the truth was he just wanted to prove his point, to show me why his way, keeping us a secret, is the right way. I disagreed so I left."

Pippa gasped. "You just left him sitting there on his own?"

"I absolutely did! It was the only thing left to do." The expression on his face had been filled with discomfort and accusation, as if I'd done something to him. "It was the only way to get him to stop looking at me as if I was the one asking for the white dress and gold ring."

Pippa nodded while she thought, her gaze fixed on a spot just over my shoulder. "What did he say afterwards?"

"Nothing. I haven't spoken to him since I left the restaurant, and I don't expect to, not for a while." We were over. Completely over before we ever really got started.

"And you're not willing to have a lowkey, off the radar relationship?"

"To what end, Pippa? So I can spend time alone with him and let my life pass me by? No way."

"Pass you by? Aren't you being just a tad dramatic?"

I shook my head. "Not at all. What happens down the line? He wants to get engaged and keep it a secret? A courthouse wedding with a handful of witnesses? Having our babies in Nashville so no one knows about it? Where will it end?" I knew that all of that was jumping the gun, but giving in to secrecy now meant I might have to accept it forever. "That's not the life I want."

"And you shouldn't accept it," she agreed. "I'm just really bummed about this. I'm so sorry honey."

"Thank you." I shrugged off the lingering sadness and flashed a smile that started to feel genuine. "I'm old enough to be used to relationships not working out," I assured her.

"True, but you care about him, and knowing nothing can come of it sucks, for that I'm sorry." She smiled again when Ryanna's baby babble kicked up a notch and she patted my shoulder as if trying to get my attention. "So what movie are we watching today anyway?"

I shrugged. "Who knows? Margot is on the committee, so probably something sappy and romantic." We shared a laugh, all talk of Chase put aside for the rest of the day.

"Let's hope it's not *Gone With The Wind*, because I totally wouldn't put it past Margot." Pippa rolled her eyes. "I mean it's a great movie and all, but I'd like something a little more upbeat and modern."

"You mean something like *Notting Hill*?" I asked about one of her favorite romantic comedy films.

"Yes. Or *Love, Actually*. Even something old school like *Pretty in Pink*." She sighed and shook her head as she reached for another date. "Damn these are so good I might have to hit the treadmill later today."

"How about I come over and we do some yoga together? I could use it too."

"Deal," she smiled, but her grin slowly faded and I didn't need to turn around to know why. Chase was here, in the park. I felt the way the air charged behind me, the way the sun seemed to get a little hotter, exponentially brighter. "Don't look now, but Chase is here."

Of course he was here. "He's the mayor, I figured he would show up."

"With a picnic basket and blanket of his own?" The

look on her face told me he was headed right towards us. "He's setting up behind you."

"Of course he is," I mumbled because there was nothing to be done about it. I could draw more attention to myself by leaving, but I didn't want to, and I refused to run the other way just because we didn't work out as a couple. "It'll be fine," I assured Pippa because she needed it. She didn't want her wedding ruined by the tension between us, and I wouldn't let that happen.

"Hey Pip!" His voice sounded behind me, happy and upbeat.

"Hey Chase," she smiled. "How's it going?"

"It's a lovely day for a movie in the park," he told her, his tone unbothered, as if nothing at all was wrong. Then again, maybe nothing was wrong. "Mind if I set up here?"

Yes.

"No," Pippa answered easily. "What's in your basket?"

"Fried chicken and potato salad, of course. And brownies, courtesy of Alice and Mabel." His tone was normal, not a hint of strain, and I willed myself not to look back, not to confirm that he was perfectly fine with the way things had played out between us. I listened as Chase spread out his blanket and unpacked his basket, hoping one of the nosy townsfolk would steal his attention away.

No such luck, however. Where were the busybodies

when you actually needed them? Chase stood in front of our blanket with a smile. "Hi Carlotta."

"Chase," I said primly as he knelt in front of me.

"Mind if I hold her?"

"She's your niece," I answered and practically shoved the baby into his arms, anything to get him away from me. And fast.

"How are you?" He was close when he asked the question, securing Ryanna in his corded arms.

"Fine. You?"

"I've been better," he said as a slow, sad smile spread across his face. "You look good."

"Thanks. So do you." He did look good in his casual jeans and t-shirt, an unbuttoned sweater clung to his biceps and I looked away.

When it became clear that I wouldn't engage him in any further conversation, Chase sighed and stood up with Ryanna. "All right. I'll be over here if you need me."

When he was gone, Pippa stared at me, trying to communicate silently, but I couldn't figure it out and I didn't bother trying. "This is the perfect setting for romance," she whispered.

"It is. Too bad Ryan isn't back yet."

"Smart ass," she shot back with a teasing smile.

"Thanks, I try." We sat in an oppressive silence for a long moment before I ended it with talk of wedding plans. "Did you pick a dress yet?"

"I did, but I refuse to buy it until I'm certain I can fit

into a size eight again." I laughed, and then she laughed. "I still need shoes and undergarments, will you come shopping with me?"

I frowned. "Don't you want Valona to do that?"

She nodded. "I was thinking we could make it a girls' day type of thing. Champagne for you guys and a mocktail for me, shopping and drooling over wedding dresses."

"Sounds perfect," I told her because it did. I could use some time with my friends, even if they were both blissfully coupled up.

"Oh my god, is this your niece?" Chase's assistant, CJ's voice cooed behind me, and I tried hard not to cringe. "Isn't she just beautiful?"

I tried hard not to roll my eyes, but in the end, I failed. It was clear to me that CJ had a crush on her boss, and whether or not Chase was oblivious to it no longer mattered to me. Maybe CJ wanted him badly enough to submit to his terms, and if so, I wished them both luck.

"What in the hell is going on?" Pippa mouthed the question to me quietly, shock in her eyes.

"No clue," I answered back, lifting one shoulder and letting it fall carelessly.

"You know she's into him, right?"

I nodded. "I'd have to be blind to miss it."

"And you don't care?"

I shook my head and echoed my earlier words to him.

"Bull," she growled. "You don't want to fight."

Maybe she was right. "Maybe there's nothing to fight for." Thankfully, Margot stood in front of the giant projector screen and the event got under way, preventing Pippa from pushing the conversation forward.

The movie started and provided the perfect distraction, though I was painfully aware of the twosome to my left sharing a picnic basket like a happy couple. I refused to look at them, but it was difficult not to notice every little movement, which mostly consisted of CJ scooting closer to Chase.

And Chase allowing it to happen.

Ryanna started to get fussy and Pippa stood. "I think that's our cue to leave," she said regretfully.

"I'll take her if you want to stay and finish the movie?"

"That's sweet Carlotta, thanks, but it's probably best if we get out of here just in case she decides to show off her lungs."

I laughed and nodded. "Let me pack up and I'll be right behind you. Go." I shooed Pippa off with Ryanna, who still hadn't quite started crying, but the little girl was working her way up to it.

"Thanks," she said and rushed off, leaving me to pack up the basket, fold the blanket and shove all of Ryanna's toys into the oversized diaper bag. I looked around to make sure I hadn't forgotten anything and my gaze connected with Chase's.

He offered up an awkward smile that I refused to return. He could pretend he didn't want CJ practically snuggled up beside him, but he did nothing to discourage it.

I was starting to wonder if I'd been completely wrong about him, maybe he was just like the other men, he just wrapped himself in good guy packaging.

Whatever, I told myself. *It doesn't matter.*

With that thought, I looked away from Chase and from the past, from the *what ifs* and *what could have beens*, I left the park, and Chase, behind.

For good.

CHAPTER 24
CHASE

What in the hell was CJ doing, sitting on my blanket uninvited? She'd helped herself to my picnic basket, and she kept sliding across the blanket to get closer to me. Why on earth was my assistant doing everything in her power to ruin my night? Didn't the woman know she was interfering with what could be my last chance to get Carlotta to remain in my life?

I kept my gaze focused on the rom-com playing out on the giant projector in the middle of the park, determined to ignore whatever it was CJ thought she might accomplish tonight.

Carlotta had done her best to ignore me since I showed up, telling me what I already knew about her feelings. She was done with me, and it was my own damn fault. In hindsight I could see how terrible the date had truly been, and it had nothing to do with the well-meaning citizens of Carson Creek and their nosy ways. It was me. All me.

I was the one who misbehaved, who took normal small town conversation as suggestion or demands. People in Carson Creek, especially the older folks, were marriage minded. They were planning weddings and babies for every new couple who appeared in public. I knew that, and still I let it get to me. I ruined my chance to show Carlotta that I was a good man, one who would do whatever it took to please his woman.

Instead, I'd driven her away.

But tonight was meant to be my shot at redemption. I'd brought some Lynchburg Lemonade because she mentioned how much she enjoyed sipping it with her mama during the oppressively hot summers in Mississippi. And now CJ sipped it straight from the bottle, effectively throwing a wrench in my peace offering, dammit. I knew I would have to have a talk to CJ—soon—about her flirtatious and presumptuous behavior, but tonight was about Carlotta. About us.

When Pippa stood with a regretful look, I sat up a little taller, knowing my chance to talk with Carlotta was close. But that moment was slowly slipping away as she started to pack up the picnic basket and the blanket, and then all of Pippa and Ryanna's stuff.

It's now or it's never, Chase.

Carlotta stood and her gaze swept over the spot

where the blanket had been, and for one brief moment, our gazes locked. She was so damn beautiful it hurt to look at her knowing I'd lost her. Not just lost, but I'd pushed her away. But when she looked away, I realized something important. She was hurt because she cared. She was angry because it mattered to her, I mattered to her. She wasn't ambivalent about me, and that was something I could work with.

"Carlotta, wait up." I jumped to me feet, determined to go after her.

She stopped and turned to me just as CJ reached out to grab my hand. "Where are you going Chase?"

I frowned down at CJ and her overly familiar behavior before I extricated my fingers from hers. "What are you doing?" I looked back at Carlotta and found that she'd already gone. Dammit. "Well?" I growled at CJ, angry that she'd stood in my way once again when it came to Carlotta.

CJ sat a little taller and pushed her chest out, giving me a view straight down her tiny sundress. "I wanted to invite you over to my place once the movie is over and you've finished your mayoral duties for the night." She purred the words, the suggestion clear in them, but I needed her intentions to be clear before I said anything.

"What for CJ?"

She smiled up at me and then licked her lips. "So we can continue our date, of course. I have wine chilling in the fridge and your favorite, chocolate cake."

Chocolate cake?

"And I have a new negligee that matches your eyes perfectly." She batted her eyelashes in what was meant to be a flirty gesture, but though she was beautiful, CJ was a child.

"CJ," I started off kind and gentle, because she was young and mostly a good assistant. "This isn't a date."

She frowned. "But we're here together. You and me. We shared the basket you made and everything." Her words were almost a whine, but still, she didn't deserve my anger.

"You sat down uninvited CJ. You're a great woman, and a wonderful assistant, but I don't date my employees." There, that was clean and painless.

"Fine. I quit."

Dammit, I should have expected that. "CJ, I don't want you to quit. You're my best assistant to date."

"But," she began again as tears welled in her eyes. "We get along so well. You're hot and I'm hot, we could be really hot together."

Her tears made this impossibly difficult, but it had to be done. "We do get along well CJ, but I'm afraid my heart already belongs to someone else." As I said the words, I knew they were true.

"But you didn't even bring *her* as your date," she spat out the words and pointed to the now empty spot previously occupied by Carlotta.

"A stupid mistake on my part, which I was trying to

correct until you showed up. Now," I straightened to standing and sighed. "If you'll excuse me, there's somewhere else I should be." I walked off in the direction Carlotta had gone, hoping she hadn't already disappeared.

"I'll drop this stuff at your place," she called out to me, her words more of a threat than a kind gesture.

I should have gone back to retrieve my belongings then and there, but I was too focused on finding Carlotta to make things right before it was too late. I should have known it wouldn't be that easy.

Alice and Mabel blocked my path first. "Mayor Carson, we hope you enjoyed the brownies. They're Mama's favorite recipe."

I smiled as best I could. "They were wonderful, and I'm sure everyone in town would happily pay for them."

They flashed matching delighted smiles and Mabel set a hand on my arm. "We'll see about that after next month's bake sale."

Another town activity I hadn't thought of because it was more than a month away. If CJ really did quit, I'd have to replace her immediately, or risk upending my entire schedule. "You know I'm rooting for you. Both of you." I had no idea if they would compete together as one entrant, or against one another.

"We won't keep you," Alice whispered. "Carlotta went that way."

"Thanks." My shoulders dropped in relief and I took

off again, anxious to get to Carlotta because I knew it would take some convincing to get her to talk to me.

"Oh Chase, there you are." Margot popped up in front of me, dressed in a pink dress that looked better suited to an office than a park. "We need to talk."

I nodded. "Do we need to talk right now, or can it wait until Monday?"

Margot's shoulders fell. "It would be better to speak about it now."

I sighed and avoided the urge to pinch the bridge of my nose. "Okay, what is it?"

"You can't let Carlotta use Grady's Bar as an event space. It's unseemly," she said, unable to suppress a disgusted shiver.

"Okay. Why not?"

"Because," she whined. "It reflects poorly on the town. You don't want strangers coming to Carson Creek thinking *that* is all we have to offer. Do you? Do you?" She asked again, her voice growing more irritated by the second.

"Margot why is this any of your business in the first place?"

She spluttered, surprised at the question. "Because we do business together, and people will wonder what's wrong with The Olde Country House if she's using a filthy bar instead." Arms folded, chin stuck high in the air, she stared at me, waiting for me to cave.

"It's her business to do with as she pleases. The bar

is a commercial space, and she has every right to use it if Grady agrees."

"But Chase, this is a joint venture."

"You aren't her boss Margot."

"No," she sighed. "I'm not."

"Then what is the problem?" I knew Margot and Grady didn't get along, but this was something more than that. "You don't have to attend events held at the bar."

"I know," she sighed and her shoulders fell. "If you're not willing to help, I'll figure something out on my own." She stomped off and I made a mental note to talk to Grady this week, but right now my focus was on finding Carlotta.

By the time I arrived at the place where Pippa had parked, her car was gone and there was no trace of Carlotta. I could have doubled back through the park and past CJ to get my car, but it would be quicker to walk the few blocks to Carlotta's place.

It wasn't dark, dammit. It was too early for her to have gone to bed already, which meant she wasn't home. My shoulders fell. I was defeated, but I wasn't ready to throw in the towel just yet. There were a few places in town she could be, so I decided to search them.

All of them.

CHAPTER 25
CARLOTTA

"Here's to sleeping in the middle of the bed again!" A round of loud cheers went up in the corner of Grady's Bar where Sandee, the divorcee, made her toast.

"Here's to never having to make acai bowls ever again!" One of her friends offered up another toast and the crowd went wild.

I couldn't help but smile at the fun Sandee was having with her friends in the corner, while the rest of the party raged on around them. I sat at the bar with a sparkling water, keeping an eye on things. It wasn't my typical event, in that I was more relaxed and there was no reason to rush around because it was all handled.

"Thanks for the booking Carlotta, the money is awesome, but let me tell you, I could do without all the ass grabbing." Grady paused at the bar. "Maybe you can tell them I'm not on the menu?"

I laughed and shook my head at his put upon expression. "I could, but where's the fun in that? Besides, I saw you eyeballing that curvy redhead with Sandee." I nodded over my left shoulder in the direction of said redhead.

Grady's grin came slow and easy as he shrugged. "What? I enjoy beautiful things, that's all. I like looking at you, but I haven't made a move, have I?"

Good point. "Thanks for that Grady." His compliment, though totally platonic, was the ego boost I desperately needed in that moment.

He frowned and stared at me for a long minute. "You need me to kick someone's ass for you? I'm happy to help out a friend, and more so with the fee you arranged for this place. Hell, I'll even throw in a few knees to the nuts if you want."

I threw my head back and laughed. "Thanks for the offer, but that's not necessary." I might still be a little sad at the way things with Chase had played out, but two weeks have passed since the picnic in the park, and we haven't spoken. The plans for Pippa and Ryan's wedding were done, the date was set and the invitations had been sent out. By next week I would have a head count. Everything was progressing nicely.

"Seriously," Grady said, his smile faded into sympathy. "For what it's worth, the mayor is an idiot if he doesn't see how great you are, or how lucky he is that you even looked in his direction."

"Thank you for saying that, but it's not that simple. And honestly I'm sick of talking about it. But you know what I'm not sick of?"

Grady arched a thick fiery brow in question.

"I'm not sick of drinking about it. Whiskey on the rocks, please and thank you." I smiled, but my heart squeezed at the thought that maybe, just maybe, Chase had a small point. The town was nosy, and everyone had noticed that we weren't spending time together, and they of course commented on it, questioned it and offered up sympathy. But that was the best part of living in Carson Creek, everyone knew everyone ,and most of all, they gave a damn. I wouldn't trade that kind of love and care for anything in the world.

"You're drinking on the clock? That doesn't sound like you're fine with things."

I shrugged. "The event is almost over, and there are very few decorations to take down," I told him as I looked around at the black and silver balloons that wished Sandee a 'Happy Divorce'. It would take ten minutes maximum, which meant I deserved a drink. "Whiskey me, barkeep!"

Grady's lips twitched before he nodded and poured three fingers of whiskey over a giant ice cube. "Barkeep?"

I shrugged. "I always wanted to say that, and you provided me with the perfect opportunity."

"I don't mind it," he whispered. "Just don't make it a habit."

"More shots, bartender!" Sandee shouted over the jukebox and licked her lips at the sight of Grady's big, tattooed body. "Buttery nipples all around."

He slid a look at me and giggled. "Still worth the money you got me for this. Drink that slowly," he ordered and went to the other end of the bar, presumably to get started on a dozen buttery nipples.

"Make them all doubles," she shouted when he began pouring.

I laughed at the grunt Grady let out, but he was a good sport about it, even though her amended order meant he'd have to start pouring the schnapps again. "Coming right up, ladies!"

"Woooo!" The collective shout of excitement tugged a smile across Grady's face.

"Is he yours?" The question came from the curvy redhead, and I smiled up at her and shook my head.

"Grady and I are friends, that's all."

"You sure?"

"Yep. Positive. He's single as far as I know."

"Yeah?" She purred the word as the corners of her lips curled into a knowing smile. "Thanks honey, and this is a great party by the way."

"Thanks sugar, be sure to tell your friends." The

words mostly hit her back as she sauntered to the other end of the bar where Grady placed the double shots on a tray.

Two and a half hours later, the bar was empty except for me and Grady. The decorations were packed into a large plastic bin by the door, and my heels sat on top of them, a pair of hot pink sneakers on my aching feet. "I'd say tonight went well. Really well."

Grady grunted as he stood beside me and stared at the pristine bar. "It did," he finally agreed, though reluctantly.

"You did good tonight, but I am sorry about the groping."

He raised one shoulder nonchalantly. "They were harmless. Energetic but harmless."

"Does that mean you won't accept any bachelorette parties here?"

"Hell no," he growled. "Bring it on. Like I said, the money is too good to pass up, and they're just having a good time. It's all in good fun."

I stared up at him, a shocked expression on my face. "Oh my God, you *like* the attention."

"I do not," he shot back in a low, gravelly voice.

"You do! You totally do!" I doubled over with laughter and shook my head as his cheeks turned pink in the dim bar.

"If you stay here another minute, I'm going to charge

you for a second day," he growled and gave me a gentle shove out the door. "I'll walk you to your car."

"You don't need to do that Grady. This is Carson Creek."

He nodded and locked the bar's front door, grabbing my plastic bin as if I hadn't just said a word. "Which way?" I pointed to where my car sat, alone under a still burning streetlight. "So what went wrong with you and the mayor?"

I groaned and shook my head. "You're as bad as the old women in town." He laughed and waited me out, damn him. "It's nothing as dramatic as people think. We just want different things in life, that's all."

"Bullshit," he spat. "You two are the definition of the marrying kind, so help me understand what the hell that means?"

I shook my head. "Would you be with a woman who wanted to keep you a secret?"

"In general? No, but I have dated a few married women who required that. If there were real feelings involved though, hell no I wouldn't accept that."

I smiled. "Then you get it."

Grady's feet stopped moving and he turned to me with a dark scowl. "That prick. I'll kick his ass whether you want me to or not."

"Thanks Grady, you really are a sweetheart under all those muscles and tattoos." I kissed his cheek and opened the back door so he could put the bins in the car.

"But don't beat up the mayor, it's bad for your business. Okay?"

He nodded and waited until I started the engine and pulled away before he turned in the opposite direction and presumably made his way home. I only wondered if the redhead waited for him somewhere.

At least someone might be getting orgasms tonight. After a long week that featured four different events, I was too tired to even consider sex, even if there was someone to fill that role in my life. I dragged my exhausted body from the Escalade, stacked the plastic bins with my purse on top, and trudged up to my porch.

I screamed in fear at the movement to my left, which sent my purse tumbling to the porch. "Dammit."

"Sorry, it's just me."

Chase. "What are you doing here, and why are you lurking around my property in the dark?"

"I wasn't lurking, I was sitting on the chair over there. Why isn't your porch light on at this time of night?"

I sighed and set down the bins to grab my purse. "I don't answer to you. Now tell me what you're doing here?"

He raked a nervous hand through his hair and down his face. "I was hoping we could talk."

"There's nothing to talk about Chase and even if there was, it might have been worth talking about last week or the week before. Not tonight."

He nodded. "I understand that, I do. But I needed some time to figure out what to say to you, and to do that, I had to figure out some stuff in my head." I stared and waited for him to continue. "There's nothing going on with me and CJ."

I held up a hand to stop his words. "I don't need to hear it, and you certainly don't owe me an explanation. If she gives you what you want, then I'm happy for you Chase."

"She's not what I want," he shot back angrily.

"I'm sorry to hear that," I said and brushed past him to get to my front door, unlocking it quickly in an effort to get away from this man and this conversation. I turned to grab the bins but Chase already had one in his hands. "I didn't ask for help."

"You don't have to ask, not ever." I knew he meant those words, yet they provided me no comfort. "I would like you to give me, give us another chance."

My eyes bugged out of my head, at least that's how it felt as his words fell like a bomb between us. "I'm sorry, I must have heard wrong."

Chase set the plastic bins down and took a step forward, his gaze serious, his green eyes dark and foreboding. "You heard me. I want us to give this another chance."

"Well if that's what *you* want, then I guess it has to happen doesn't it?" My words were as sarcastic as they could be. "Why would I agree to this when it would change absolutely nothing?"

"You don't know that."

"Oh, but I do. At first I thought this was all about your privacy, like you said, about some sense of having something just for yourself. But that's not it at all. You're just like every other man on the planet, terrified of commitment. Your position as mayor just gives you a better excuse than most."

"That's not true," he insisted. "You saw what they were like!"

"Yeah, I did. They were too curious and incredibly nosy, just like always. I don't know why you think you get to be exempt as mayor. These people care about the people of this town and they want them to be happy, plain and simple. No one is forcing you to get married or even get serious if you don't want to, but that's the point isn't it? You don't actually want to."

"Don't say that," he growled, his voice as angry as the expression on his face.

"Look Chase, I get it, the truth is difficult to hear, and damn near impossible to accept. But we can't change who we are or what we want in life."

He took another step closer and heat flared in his eyes. A beat later his arms wrapped around my waist and pull my body flush against his, hard and sculpted. "There's something else we can't change, Carlotta, this heat that swirls between us whenever we're together." A grin split his face a moment before his mouth crashed down on mine, practically drowning me in the heat and desire he offered.

I wanted to resist, wanted to pretend his kissed did nothing for me, but I couldn't. Instead of resisting, I dove in head first, consequences be damned.

For now, anyway.

CHAPTER 26
CHASE

As soon as our lips touched, all of the oxygen fled the room. It was difficult to breathe, to find one extra breath of air, because I was so consumed by the feel of her plump lips against mine, the tangy taste of some kind of alcohol mixed with chocolate or something sweet. Her kisses were the only ones I wanted, the only ones that mattered, and though Carlotta gave in to the kiss, her curves pressed against my body, arms wrapped tight around me, I knew this wasn't actual capitulation.

She wasn't giving in, not yet, at least not to anything beyond this burning lust that wouldn't seem to go away. When she was around I wanted her, and if this kiss was any indication, it was the same for her. We were trapped by the fire that swirled around us, the flames licked at our bodies, threatening to incinerate everything in its path.

Sweat beaded on my forehead as her hands slid down my back in slow, drugging moves that sent shivers up and down my spine. She sucked my tongue and I damn near lost every ounce of control and willpower I'd been holding on to since she walked up her porch, beautiful and exhausted. "Carlotta," I growled and nipped her bottom lip. From one jaw to the other and then down her neck. I enjoyed every gasp and every shiver that told me she was just as into this as I was.

Maybe more.

I picked her up and tossed her onto her oversized, squishy sofa, smiling at her gasp of shock that tore into the silent room.

I kissed my way down her body and removed every stitch of clothing she had on from the little black dress to the sexy heels that showed off shapely calves and highlighted the curve of her ass. She was so damn gorgeous, I couldn't look away, and once she was bared to my gaze, it took a miracle for me to do anything other than stare at her feminine beauty.

"Chase," she moaned and tangled her fingers in my hair.

I started at her ankles and kissed my way all the way back up to her sweet, plump lips. Juicy and soft like the ripest of fruits. Our lips and tongues and teeth tangled together in a wet mess, and when she pulled back, Carlotta's eyes were glazed over and her lips were swollen from my kisses. I wanted her too badly to wait, I was too hungry to stop as I kissed between her breasts, stopping to lavish love on the bouncy flesh and the hard nubs as she squirmed and moaned beneath me.

She let out a soft throaty moan and I looked up at her with a smile.

"I've been dreaming of you for days Carlotta. Just like this." I let out a long breath and opened her to my gaze. She pulsed under the heat of my gaze or the gust of air I blew on her.

"Chase," she moaned or maybe she panted, either way the sound was like a shot of whiskey, so hot it burned.

"That's me," I growled. "Remember I'm the one who makes you feel this way." My head fell forward and there she was, hot and wet and sticky on my tongue. I licked her until she squealed, sucked on her clit until her hips bucked against my jaw. I loved on her with my mouth until she couldn't stand it and squirmed and squealed.

"Chase."

I smiled and hooked one arm and then the other behind her knees, my hands clasped hers until we were tangled up, palm to palm, completely attached in nearly every way. Taking advantage of our position and her vulnerability my tongue went back to work, swirling around her clit and thrusting deep inside her body. Over and over I licked and sucked at her core and I refused to let up until she was a quivering mess on my tongue.

"Oh!"

I smiled against her and hummed my approval, the vibrations sent her hips bucking but she couldn't move, not enough. Up and down my tongue flicked against her clit, more and more moisture gathered and dripped from her body and down my chin. When I tugged her clit into my mouth and sucked it, over and over again, she bucked and she howled as her body vibrated, quivered and shook with force of the pleasure that poured from her body.

Her body shook and I continued to lick and suck her gently, just enough to keep her on the brink of orgasm. Again. "Chase," she whimpered and that was it, that was the sound that snapped my control.

Carlotta reached out for me as I stood and rid myself of my clothes but I took a step back because I was too far gone to control myself. "I need you Car. Please."

"I'm here," she purred and opened to me.

The sight of her, pink and glistening, was more than I could stand. I knelt between her thighs and rubbed myself against her until her breath hitched and then I slid home in one deep thrust. Her body clamped around me, still pulsing from her last orgasm and my body took off like a rocket.

She was hot and so damn wet I knew I wouldn't last long, but being here with her like this was exactly what I wanted and I pounded into her, every feeling, every emotion that coursed through me in hopes that she could feel them, identify every one and somehow, just know how I felt about her.

She gasped and panted, her nails dug into my flesh and I didn't give a damn. "More Chase, please."

I withdrew and thrust forward like a man wholly consumed by his woman. She was all I could see as I poured pleasure into her and she reached up to meet me every time. I sank into her core until she shook, the rhythm between us only broken when her back arched and her ankles tightened low on my back.

"Let go for me, babe. Come for me."

Carlotta's teeth sank into her bottom lip and her eyes fluttered shut as her body tightened and froze, moisture leaking between us as her walls clamped and squeezed around me. And then she let out the longest, wildest cry of pleasure I'd ever heard.

My hips moved through her pulsing channel until my sac tightened and electricity shot up my spine, moments later I surrendered to the pleasure between us. "Oh fuck, I think I'm dead."

Her laugh was husky as one hand played in my hair, her nails scraped gently against my scalp, drawing me closer to sleep.

Not yet. We needed to talk, it was imperative that we did before she shove her feelings down deep and sent me home. "Carlotta," I whispered and nibbled her earlobe.

"Chase," she moaned as her pussy still pulsed around me. "That was nice," she purred.

Nice? "Give me another chance and we can be nice like this together again and again." I dragged my teeth across her collarbone, loving the way I could make her feel so good with just a small move.

She gasped with pleasure, but she now held herself back, denied me. "To what end, Chase?"

I drew a nipple between my teeth and sucked hard. "That end. We can give each other so much pleasure, both in and out of the bedroom," I moaned and moved to her other breast. "Just give us another chance." I lost myself for a moment in the taste of her, the hard nub of her nipples covered in silky flesh, the way her pleasure oozed where we were still connected.

"Okay," she moaned.

I froze and pulled back. "Okay?"

She nodded and settled her dark gaze on my face as if she was searching for something. "Okay. I'll give us another try if you agree to be my date for Pippa's wedding."

It was a simple request in the grand scheme of things, I knew that. On an intellectual level I knew that, but the question itself caused me to freeze and all the blood drained from my face. My mind raced and whirled with the thought of the entire town interrupting every bite of short ribs, every dance and every conversation with some quip about what a beautiful bride Carlotta would make. How she would make a fantastic mother and the perfect political wife. My throat closed up as image after image appeared in my mind, stealing all the joy I should feel when my only sister finally married the love of her life.

Carlotta misunderstood my silence, and she pushed at my chest until our bodies separated and I was on the other side of the sofa. She grabbed up her clothes and held them in front of her, more of a shield than any attempt at modesty.

"That's exactly what I thought Chase. Trying again sounds good, in theory, but the problem is you don't actually want to try. You want me to accept what you're offering and give up what I want completely."

"That's not true," I said as my shoulders fell in defeat. "I just want to enjoy being with you."

"Yeah, like this. In private. No thanks," she whispered almost inaudibly. "This," she motioned between our naked bodies, "Is all that we can ever be Chase and this was it. The last time." With tears welling in her eyes, she turned away from me and hurried up the stairs. A few seconds later the shower started and I stood and picked up my clothes.

I took my time getting dressed, hoping I could see her again, make one last argument for us. But five minutes later the shower was still going, and I knew she wouldn't come out until she was sure I was gone.

For good this time.

CHAPTER 27
CARLOTTA

"Well ladies, what do you think?" Pippa stepped from the fitting room in sexy all-white lingerie. "Does this look like it'll drive Ryan wild?"

Valona tossed her head back and laughed, a glass of champagne in her hand, her face lit with love and happiness. "If that's your goal, save the cash and wear nothing. But yes, you look hot as hell in that."

Pippa's blue eyes turned to me. "And you, wedding planner extraordinaire, what's the verdict?"

"With your figure you can make just about anything look fantastic, but maybe don't go for white?"

Pippa frowned. "Are you maligning my purity?"

"Absolutely," I joked. "No, I just mean that a very light shade of purple or blue, even a pale yellow would take the sex appeal up a notch."

Pippa thought about it for a long time as she examined her reflection with a soft smile. "Maybe you're right," she said and disappeared back inside the fitting room.

Valona and I sat on a plush sofa on our first stop for this girls' day excursion. The lingerie shop specialized in wedding undergarments, and the more I sat there surrounded by shades of white and pastel, surrounded by reminders of love and happy endings, the more it reminded me of what I didn't have. Might never have. It left me both depressed and hopeful.

"What's on your mind?" Valona's eyes were full of concern, and I knew I had to get her off the scent because today was about Pippa, not me and my drama.

I let out a rough laugh. "What's not on my mind? Just keeping a running tally of all the things I need to do for upcoming events." The barn was being decorated at this moment, and even though Margot was more than capable, my stomach clenched at not being there to supervise it myself. My assistant was handling the ballroom for another upcoming event, and my mind really was swirling with all that had to be done.

"Relax Carlotta, this is meant to be a fun day for all of us." She wrapped an arm around me and laid her head on my shoulder. "I'm sorry about you and Chase. I thought you were a really cute couple."

"Thanks. I'm sorry too, but I'm also used to it, you know?" Dating at my age was difficult enough without getting heartbroken over the end of every *almost* relationship.

"Believe me, I know." She too had given up on love until she'd met a gorgeous younger man determined to win her over. "But the right man won't stop at anything to have you, to be in your life."

"I know. I was there, remember?" My words drew a laugh from both of us. But I knew what she was saying, Chase clearly wasn't the man for me, since he wasn't willing to do anything outside of his comfort zone to make room for me in his life. "The disappointment will pass."

"It always does," she sighed and took my glass to refill them both. "Can I say how happy I am that Ryan got us a driver for the day? Now that man is a keeper."

I drained the champagne and smacked my lips. "Amen to that sister."

"All right ladies, how about this one?" Pippa stood in a pale pink lace set that was sexy and just edgy enough for a rock star. The bralette and panties wrapped around in a crisscross pattern that made it look as if it were a one-piece.

"Damn woman, you are *gorgeous*," Valona said breathlessly.

I nodded my agreement. "Sexy and feminine, with just a hint of color. Ryanna's going to have a sibling sooner rather than later."

"You think so?" Her excited eyes were so happy, I felt tears sting the back of my eyes.

Valona and I both nodded our agreement. "Definitely," I told her. "That's the one."

"Perfect!" Pippa performed an excited toe-tap dance in a circle and she did a little shimmy. "Thank you ladies so much, and now," she banged her fingers against her thigh and made a drumroll noise with her mouth. "I'm buying you lingerie. In solidarity."

I laughed. "Solidarity lingerie. Is that a thing?"

Valona shrugged. "Apparently, and I for one don't plan on turning down free, fancy and super sexy lingerie" She pushed off the plush sofa with the grace of a dancer and started browsing.

"And I never look a gift horse in the mouth, whatever that really means," I said and took my time searching for the perfect lingerie set that was sexy enough to boost my confidence, even though no one was likely to see it anytime soon.

As I browsed through racks and racks of over the top, completely impractical sleepwear, I wondered if there were some comfy white flannel pajamas for older couples on their wedding day.

Eventually Pippa's eyelids grew heavy and it was time to head to the next destination, which was perfect, because I was definitely in the mood for good food and plenty of wine.

Lots and lots of wine.

When we arrived at the reserved room inside Dark Horse, the party had already started without the bride-to-be. Lacey and Margo sat talking quietly over big glasses of wine, red for Lacey and white for Margo. Lacey's soon-to-be daughter in law Michelle, arrived soon after we did, and she wore an uncertain smile.

"Honey, your goal for the next year is to make more friends," I whispered in Pippa's ear before we joined the party.

"No kidding. How sad and pathetic is this?" Pippa's shoulders fell and I rubbed encouraging circles on her back. "I spent so much time working over the past couple decades that I didn't take the time to foster real friendships.

I shrugged and wrapped an arm around Pippa's waist. "That's all right. More booze, and more of Nina's delicious food just for us."

"I like the sound of that," she shot back, stood taller and strode forward to get her bridal shower party started. "Ladies, I'm so glad you could join me to celebrate my impending nuptials."

Margot stood, the very picture of southern elegance as she smoothed the sides of her peach dress and checked to make sure her pearls were straight. "Pippa, I wouldn't miss this celebration for the world. You and Ryan have a love story for the ages, only strengthened by the fact that it took decades for us to arrive here. It gives the rest of us hope." Margot pulled Pippa in for an uncharacteristically emotional hug. "I'm thrilled for you."

Pippa blinked, surprised by Margot's show of emotion. "Thank you, Margot."

Margot pulled back, seeming to remember who she was as she stood a little taller. "My pleasure. And we have sparkling cider chilling on ice for the guest of honor."

Pippa took her seat and the rest of us gathered at the table around her as dish after dish was brought out, and a steady stream of alcohol filtered into the room. It was as perfect as things could get when the party planner was also a guest, and I mentally clapped myself on the back at the good job I'd done planning everything out.

At least I'm still good at my job.

I settled into my seat and allowed myself to relax, to enjoy being in the room with these incredible women I was lucky enough to call my friends. The wine flowed and I soaked up the laughter around me as Pippa opened up gifts, both useful and totally inappropriate.

"You girls are really trying to make sure I return from my honeymoon pregnant, aren't you?" Pippa laughed at the package of edible underwear and slipped them into her purse with a knowing grin.

"If nothing else," Lacey said above the roar of laughter that erupted from the room, "you'll have lots of fun practicing."

"Obviously," Pippa added with another smile.

"Thank you ladies, for all of your wonderful and wild gifts. Ryan and I will enjoy them all and think of you fondly."

"Oh geez, leave it to Pippa to turn a gift into a threesome," Valona joked good-naturedly.

"We all have our super powers," she shot back with a proud smile.

Eventually talk turned from the wedding and the wedding night to men in general. I held my breath and kept my focus on my bottomless glass of merlot.

"You're awfully quiet Carlotta." I should have known the reporter wouldn't let my subdued behavior go by unnoticed. "Are you nursing a broken heart?"

"Nope. I'm not." I'd moved quickly through the pain portion of the break up and straight into anger and frustration. Those were stages of grief, weren't they?

"Oh please," Pippa offered up with an eyeroll. "You and Chase are adorable together. You're good together, but you both are too damn stubborn for your own good."

"It's not about being stubborn," I insisted with more energy than I should have around this group. "It's just realizing that you don't want the same things, so it doesn't matter how much you want each other. End of discussion." It was a hopeful way to end the conversation, but I knew it wouldn't work.

"Not *end of discussion*," Pippa mimicked with a playful smile. She looked around the room to each woman and gave them a quick rundown of my relationship with Chase and its premature demise. "I think she should give him another chance."

"Your opinion is not exactly unbiased Pippa. And there's nothing to fight for. He wants a relationship in secret, and I don't. I'm not going to fight for a one-sided relationship. Chase doesn't want me enough to risk anything, which is basically the same as saying he doesn't want *me* enough. It hurts, but it's the truth, and I can live with that." Despite the increasing ache in my heart at laying myself open like that, I knew it would pass.

Eventually.

"Maybe you ought to just show him how great it can be," Margot offered.

"Tried that, and it was an unmitigated disaster. He doesn't want to share that part of his life with the town, and I won't hide in the shadows."

Lacey nodded. "I get it. You spend all of your time in a romantic love bubble, only for him to up and decide you're not the woman for him, and you've wasted your time and energy."

"Exactly. But more than that, I'm not exactly the hiding type. I live my life out in the open. Period." I held up a glass while the server refilled it. "To the top," I encouraged with a smile. "I appreciate the advice, but there's nothing to be done about this. It's just the way things worked out this time." And every other time, at least in my experience.

Feeling just past the point of being tipsy, I poured myself into the back of the limo and closed my eyes as I listened to the excited chatter of my friends. They were looking forward to the wedding, to getting dressed up with their gorgeous men on their arms as much as they were ready to celebrate Ryan and Pippa making their love official. Finally. My mind swirled with thoughts of my dress and the long list of tasks I needed to accomplish before wedding.

My thoughts were most definitely *not* on the town's mayor and his piercing green eyes. Or his strong arms.

Nope, not at all.

CHAPTER 28
CHASE

I *should have brought Carlotta as my date.*

That was the first thought that popped into my head as I entered the beautifully decorated barn alone, sandwiched between laughing and flirting twosomes. Not only would having her by my side make the wedding and the entire evening ahead much more enjoyable, but dammit I just missed her.

As soon as the crowd ahead of me parted in search of their tables, I spotted her, and she was even more gorgeous than usual. Instead of her go-to black or navy blue dress, her curves were draped in slinky gold fabric that highlighted her sun-kissed skin, and I knew if I were closer I'd see the freckles on her shoulders. Her dark hair was swept into one of those intricate updo styles with sexy tendrils hanging down, brushing her cheeks and collarbone, making my fingers itch to bridge the gap between us and touch her. She looked stunning.

And I lost her.

We hadn't spoken since that mind-blowing night where I couldn't agree to take her as my date to the wedding. She no longer needed my input on wedding details, so she hadn't reached out, and neither had I. A mistake I deeply regretted at the moment.

A hand landed harsh on my shoulder and pulled me from my musings, pulled my attention reluctantly from Carlotta and to my new brother-in-law. "She's looking good enough to eat isn't she?" Roman asked the question casually, but his gaze held a little too much heat for my liking, and I frowned in his direction. Rock star or not, Carlotta was mine, or she would be as soon as I figured out how to win her back. Roman laughed at my expression. "No offense bro, I heard how you messed up things with her, but I'm not getting in your way Chase, just stating a fact."

I nodded, because he was right, she did look good enough to eat. I snorted at my own silliness and turned to Roman. "How's the album coming along?"

"All done," he answered with a proud grin. "It turns out I can be both a solo artist and a member of The Gregory Brothers, especially with their support and blessing. Hey, I guess you're my brother now too."

I flashed an amused grin. "That's how this works, but you're still the baby, and I'm not a rock star."

"I don't know man, you're kind of a rock star aren't you? I mean that's why you want to keep everything with Carlotta hush-hush right?" There was a hint of a smile as he spoke, and I sent my elbow into his side. "Too soon?"

"Way too soon," I growled at him. I was living with the consequences of my actions, only it didn't feel like living at all, more like I was coping with the consequences. Learning to live without Carlotta, dammit. "Yeah I messed it up but I didn't realize it until I went back to living without her. How can one person make such an impact in such a short period of time?"

Roman let out a huff of laughter that held no trace of humor. "It tends to sneak up on you like that."

A passing server stopped in front of us. "Signature cocktail? Champagne or beer?" Her words were for both of us, but her gaze ate up Roman.

"Tell me about the cocktails," he drawled, lips quirked into a small smile.

"We have Pippa's Garden, which features a lavender gin and lemonade. The Happy Ending is a cross between a whiskey smash and a mint julep."

"Happy Ending," we both said at the same time, plucking two glasses from the tray.

I took a sip and let my gaze wander the barn until I spotted the woman painted with liquid gold, and then I took another sip as the ache of losing her gripped my heart.

"You know, I was scared as hell to strike out on my own, wondered if I had what it took without my brothers to back me up. I was even more terrified to tell them, but it all worked out for the best. Ryan has even more money coming in from the songwriting, so there's not the same pressure to tour now that he's started a family. Derek gets to do more producing now while I do my thing. All that fear for nothing."

"Hmm," was my only response as I watched Carlotta smile and laugh with the wedding attendees.

"My point is," Roman said, his deep voice forcing my attention back to him, "is that getting the fuck out of your comfort zone can be rewarding. This town is nosy as fuck," he laughed. "That includes me, I'm here at your side all up in your business, but they care. A lot. If you need signatures to declare something a historical landmark, fundraisers for re-election, or people to pick up leaves for the older homeowners, all you'd have to do is ask, and they would all line up to help. And if I tell you right now that Derek is in search of a plot of land, a realtor will approach him before he made it to the other side of the barn. That's just the way it goes."

He was right, of course. It was the beauty of living in a small town as well as the curse. Everyone helped out everyone else, the whole damn town was like family, well-meaning but nosy as hell. I turned to Roman with his big blue eyes and wild blond hair, "Aren't you supposed to be the wild Gregory brother?"

He shrugged, but I didn't miss that hint of pride in his smile. "I *am* the wild one, but the other two are boring as fuck, so it's easy to be the wild one. But I'm also the gorgeous one and the wise one." He took a long sip of his drink and sighed dramatically.

I followed his gaze back to Carlotta's beautiful face, lit with excitement as she wrapped her arms around Ryanna and cuddled her. "She can do better than me."

Roman nodded beside me. "Of course she can. Pippa can do better than Ryan, but he's the one who owns her heart. He's the one she chose to love, and believe me, he feels lucky every damn day that she did. Trust me, I've heard the songs. That's just how it works Chase, we're never good enough for the women we love, but we work hard, every day, to become worthy of them. Right?"

"Shit," I grunted as his words sank in. "When did you get so smart too?"

He laughed and clapped me on the back again. "Song writing makes you incredibly introspective, and I've spent most of my life listening to women tell me why they like a particular set of lyrics. Life on the road is its own kind of education, Chase."

I snorted. "I received a formal education, and I feel like I got cheated out of some important lessons."

Roman laughed. "But I'm sure you can break down the societal whatever of Shakespeare or something like that."

I laughed and shook my head. "Yeah, thanks for that."

"My pleasure new brother, now if you don't mind there is a gorgeous woman over there, and surprisingly I don't know her, but I would like to. Very much." Before I answered, Roman strolled off and sidled up to the woman with deadly focus.

Time to become worthy of her.

My feet began to move in Carlotta's direction. She'd moved on from Ryanna, and now chatted with Lacey and Levi at a table near the front of the barn. I knew for a fact that my name card was at the same table, so I made a quick switch so my seat was beside hers. "Anyone need a drink? A server is headed our way."

Levi lit up with a smile. "Pippa's Garden is delicious and refreshing. You want anything, babe?"

Lacey shook her head. "I think The Happy Ending is making me dizzy," she said with a laugh.

"And you, Carlotta?" She hadn't said anything, and I knew only the direct approach would ensure good manners overrode her desire to ignore me.

"I'm fine, thanks." Her voice was civil and cool, not the warmth I usually associated with this woman.

When the server stopped at the table, I grab Pippa's Garden because the purple drink was right up Carlotta's alley. "Just in case you change your mind," I whispered softly in her ear.

"Want to dance," Levi asked Lacey clumsily.

Lacey frowned at him and pointed towards the barn doors. "The bride and groom haven't showed up yet, there is no dancing until then."

Levi's eyes widened, and he and Lacey had a minute-long silent conversation. "We don't need music to dance, do we?"

"Oh. No, we don't. Come on, then. If you play your cards right, I'll let you take advantage of me later."

Levi's deep rumbling laughter faded as they stood and left the table, giving me a moment alone with Carlotta.

"You look breathtaking tonight, Car."

"Don't," she started. "Don't come over here and talk to me like that, Chase. You could have been here with me, but you chose not to."

"I know. You're right and I was wrong. So damn wrong."

She stood abruptly. "I need to check on things before Pippa and Ryan arrive. The photos should be finished by now."

I reached out and wrapped my hand around her wrist. "Car, please. Just give me a moment. Please?"

She softened for a brief moment before she pulled back, regret shining in her eyes. "I can't Chase. I just... can't." The moment my grip loosened, she fled as if being in my presence was painful to her.

I sat there and watched her flit away in search of a reason—any reason—to get as far away from me as possible without leaving the wedding reception. A simple apology wasn't going to work, not on its own anyway. I finished my Happy Ending—what a joke—and started on Pippa's Garden, hoping the alcohol would clear my mind enough to come up with a way to win Carlotta back.

A few minutes later, the crowd grew louder as Pippa and Ryan entered, making their first appearance as husband and wife, followed by the matron of honor, Valona, and the best man Derek. Everyone was all smiles as they entered, accepted well wishes and hugs through tears and squeals of excitement.

I hated myself that I wasn't as happy on my only sister's wedding day. Pippa was finally with the man of her dreams. They were building a family and a life together here in town, and all I could think about was the sad state of my own nonexistent love life. And worse, I only had myself to blame for my current state.

I stood as Pippa and Ryan made their way to the table front and center of the barn, where their new love would be on full display for the entire town and plenty of Nashville and Hollywood musical royalty. "You look beautiful, Pip."

My sister smiled brightly and wrapped me in a tight hug. "Thanks Chase. You look handsome too, minus the sad puppy expression on your face."

I pulled back with a smile. "Despite how my face

looks, I am wildly happy for you. For both of you." I turned and shook Ryan's hand. "Welcome to the family."

Ryan wrapped his arms around Pippa and hugged her tight. "It's about damn time."

"Better late than never," I told him honestly.

"Exactly," Pippa said, a determined look in her eyes that put me on edge.

"Not today, Pip. Just enjoy your day. Eat your fill and dance until your toes hurt. Stop worrying about the rest of the world."

She hugged me again and laughed. "It's my wedding, and I'll do what want I want, baby brother."

I rolled my eyes because she had that look in her eye, the one that meant she had something up her sleeve, and no one would talk her out of whatever she had planned.

CHAPTER 29
CARLOTTA

"I'm just glad that Pippa finally put my brother out of his misery. He's not so surly, and the songs are incredible." Derek raised his glass in one hand, the microphone in the other, a wide superstar smile on his face. "Friends, family, other loved ones and business associates, raise your glasses with me to toast Mr. and Mrs. Gregory! To the happy couple." Derek smiled at the crowd and then at me as I made my way to him.

"Great job, Best Man." I reached for the microphone just as Pippa snagged it from her brother-in-law's hand. "What are you doing?" She wasn't supposed to be giving a speech. "Everything is all timed out, Pip."

She turned to me with a defiant glint in her eyes, a devilish smile on her face. "It's my wedding and I can do what I want, and right now, what I want is to give a speech. Is that all right with you?"

The bride is almost always right, I reminded myself and took a step back. "Perfectly all right."

"First, I would like to thank each and every one of you for showing up to celebrate this special day with me and Ryan. Our story took a lot longer to play out than I thought it would, but here we are. Happy and in love with each other and our beautiful little girl, Ryanna." She waved to her baby, happily cradled in her grandfather's arms. "Thank you Valona and Derek for being part of this circus with us. You both have always had a front row seat, so it was only right that you stood up with us today. I love you both."

"What about me?" Roman called the question from his seat a few feet away, drawing laughs from everyone in attendance.

"I love you too Roman, almost as much as my husband." She giggled. "My husband. I love you with every particle of my being, babe."

"And I love you with all that I am, Pip, and I'm working hard every day to be the man you and Ryanna deserve and need." His words didn't project as much without the microphone, but I heard enough to bring tears to my eyes. They were perfect together, and I couldn't be happier for my friend on this day, even if my own heart felt tattered and shredded.

Pippa looked at me with a smile and then she

turned to the table in front where Chase sat with Lacey and Levi, Roman and Trey along with their three girls. One spot, my chair, was noticeably vacant and I knew the moment Pippa spotted it, because a small frown marred her beautiful features. "And there are two more people who deserve more thanks than Ryan and I can possibly give. My brother Chase and our fabulous wedding planner, Carlotta. You two stepped in to help plan this wonderful day when we couldn't. Your help allowed me the time to learn how to be a mom while Ryan was off being a rockstar to support our family. Without the two of you, I'm not sure how this day would have happened and to show our appreciation we have a special gift for you both." She waved us both up and I shook my head.

No. She wouldn't.

The mischievous look on her face told me that yes, she would. "Come on up guys, don't be shy." She laughed and egged on the shouts and cheers from the crowd.

Reluctantly Chase and I both made our way to where Pippa stood, all smiles as she wrapped an arm around me. "What are you up to?" Chase asked, the skepticism in his tone matched the look on my face I was sure.

Pippa produced a red envelope and handed it to me. "I want you to open it up when the time is right, which only you two will know. But for now, I'd like to share our first dance with the two people who made this day happen. She stepped back and went to the bridal table where Ryan stood with heat in his eyes.

I took a step back, determined to get out of this dance however I could. It was bad event planner karma to wish for a disaster, but even that didn't stop me from straining my ears to listen for a dropped plate or something, anything to take me away from here.

Away from Chase.

He held a hand out, a sad smile on his face. "There's no getting out of this Car."

He was right and I knew it, but I didn't have to like it. With a heavy sigh, I put my hand in his and ignored the zip of attraction that served as a reminder of what I couldn't have, of what we would never be.

"Fine. Let's just do this."

Chase pulled back, surprise flashed on his face. "Is dancing with me really so terrible?"

"Yes, and no. I don't want to keep coming back to this point Chase, remembering how good we are together and why we can't be together. It hurts."

He led me a few feet away onto the dance floor and pulled me close. "I'm hurting too, Carlotta. I hurt with the ache of missing you, of knowing that the hurt I see in your eyes is because of me. That kills me."

I knew that much was true. "That's because you're a nice guy, Chase."

"I don't feel like a nice guy right now, I feel like a coward."

I shrugged in his arms. "You want what you want Chase. It doesn't make you bad, it just makes us incompatible." Knowing that and believing it were two separate things, so I kept my eyes close and danced with him, cheek to cheek, savoring these last moments in his arms. When the song ended, I pulled back with a sad smile that was about fifteen seconds from becoming watery, and I walked away.

After the world's most awkward wedding dance, I buried myself in the tasks of a proper wedding planner. The official speeches were done, Pippa and Ryan enjoyed their first dance as a married couple, and they'd danced with their respective parents before the dance floor opened up to all the partygoers.

Finally, dinner was served and I stayed busy through the meal with orders to the servers to keep my plate warm for later. Anything to avoid another painful conversation with the man who didn't think that I, or *we*, were worth fighting for. I didn't want to share a table with him or sit beside him, not because I hated him, but because it hurt too damn much.

Instead I watched from the sidelines, keeping an eye on the appetizers that Pippa insisted be served buffet style. "Hey, what's the liquor stock looking like?"

Grady looked up from where he was crouched behind the bar, a knowing smile. "Shouldn't you be sitting down to eat?"

I shrugged. "I'll eat later."

Grady unfolded his big body so he towered over me even from his spot behind the bar. "When everyone else has finished?"

I nodded defensively. "I'm working."

"Yeah, working hard at avoiding the mayor," he snorted and shook his head. "I saw that dance, you know."

"So did everyone else. What's your point?"

Grady worked quickly on a new batch of drinks and set them on the bar without ice before he started on something else altogether. "My point is that what I saw, wasn't the end of something."

I smiled. "Who knew you were a hopeless romantic?"

"I just have eyes, and I'm not emotionally invested so I see the truth."

I folded my arms. "Yeah, and what's this truth you see?"

He slid a drink across the bar with a slow smile. "Enjoy this with your dinner Carlotta. It's called Unfinished Business."

"Clever," I snorted and took the drink just as the tables started to clear as half the guests hit the dance floor. "Thanks for this." I made my way to the empty table and waved at a server on my way over.

I ate my meal like a woman starved since I hadn't eaten anything other than an apple for breakfast, and enjoyed watching the people of Carson Creek—old and young alike—give it their all on the dance floor. I couldn't help but smile as several town council members danced to the latest pop song, but watching Trey dip Valona gave my heart a squeeze.

I would likely be planning their wedding next. Or Lacey and Levi's wedding. There would always be weddings to plan, anniversary parties and baby showers, it was a good chunk of my business. Today it bothered me more than it usually did. I finished my food and pushed away from the table as an upbeat pop song ended and a slow, romantic song began.

Next came the traditional cake cutting, which made for what I knew would be really great photos.

Almost there.

After the cake cutting would come the bouquet and garter toss, and then my job would be done for the evening. I could relax since I had all day tomorrow to clean the barn with my crew.

With my *Unfinished Business* in one hand and my eyes closed, I let myself relax as the party raged on, complete with a conga line, the Electric Slide and a classic Cowboy Cha Cha. Today was a job well done and I smiled, feeling proud of myself for being able to shove aside my own heartache to give one of my oldest friends the beautiful romantic day of her dreams.

"Good job, Car."

I startled at the use of Chase's nickname for me, and my eyes flew open. Panic settled in and I wished it was about two hours later, so I could herd the bride and groom off and go home to lick my wounds.

"Excuse me, folks." Chase's deep voice sounded over the PA system and my heart sped up. "If you don't mind, I have a few things to say."

The crowd quieted down and I stood, eager, or maybe anxious to get a look at his face. "The floor is yours Mr. Mayor," someone called out. Someone who sounded a lot like Grady.

My gaze landed on Chase. He looked nervous as he wiped his free hand on his pants. He looked to Pippa, who gave him an encouraging nod and a smile. "Many of you have probably seen me around town with Carlotta Montgomery. At least for a little while."

All eyes turned to me and the crowd parted, leaving a straight line between me and Chase.

"The truth is that I messed up. Big time." He sighed and scrubbed a hand over his face. "You see, I wasn't planning on falling for her, and when it started to happen, I got scared. Really scared," he said on a huff of laughter. "When the good and inquisitive folks of this town started to comment on our future, a future that I could see laid out for myself, I did what us men tend to do. I freaked out."

Knowing chuckles sounded throughout the barn, even a few commiserative head nods went around from some of the men.

"I tried to keep this beautiful, intelligent and vibrant

woman in the shadows. If you can believe it, I asked her to keep us a secret."

"There are no secrets in Carson Creek," someone called out.

"As a lifelong resident, you would think I know that by now." He laughed good naturedly, and I felt my heart pounding in anticipation of what he would say next. "But it was an excuse because I was scared. Everyone talks about falling in love, but only the good parts, the rush of a first kiss. The way your whole body vibrates when she walks into a room." Chase's gaze ate me up and an answering heat started in the pit of my stomach. "That thrill of learning something new about someone you've known forever, and that hitch in your throat when you realize that this person, this friend was starting to become something more. That's what everyone tells you about falling in love."

"It's the best," a female voice chimed in.

Chase nodded and smiled, his gaze never leaving mine. "It is the best, but right on the heels of that comes panic and fear. That feeling that you love someone else, that you're ready to hand your heart over to them on a silver platter. And then the fear that you might lose them whether through your own stupidity, or some tragic event." He shook his head. "And that fear drove away the woman I love."

I gasped at his use, his *many* uses of the 'L' word. Love. He said he was falling in love with me, that he'd fallen in love with me, and now, just plain love. Chase said he loved me, out loud and in front of the entire Carson's Creek. I sat a little taller in my chair wondering what, if anything, it all meant.

"You see," he said, this time directly to me, "I suspected I was falling in love with you Carlotta, but when you walked away and I was forced to face the prospect of a future without you, I knew for certain that you owned my heart."

A round of *awwww's* went around the room, mostly female.

"Every day without you was just not as good as all the days with you. The sky seemed duller, the day was less exciting knowing I wasn't going to hear your laughter, to see you in one of those sexy retro dresses I've grown to love."

"Chase," his name came out on a longing whisper I wasn't even sure was audible.

But the small curve at the corners of his lips told me he'd heard me. Loud and clear. "I miss you. I missed you enough that I was forced to reexamine my own ideas and motives, and you know what I realized?"

"What's that?" Roman's voice called out from somewhere close to Chase.

"That being with you, that loving you and knowing, or maybe just hoping that you love me back, is worth everything."

"Even the questions?" I stood and folded my arms

because his words were pretty, and the fact that he was saying them here, at the biggest event this town has seen in years, meant something. But what? Did it change anything, really?

"Especially the questions." He looked around and found the Turner sisters with a smile. "It was good to do something other than work, ladies. You're right, a man like me should be married to the woman he loves with a house full of babies."

Babies? Did he just say babies, plural?

"And Mayor Riley was right too, you're the perfect woman for me in all ways, even more if I pursue politics beyond Carson Creek. Everyone else was right too, we are adorable together in the words of Belle and Bridget. Margot was right when she said I couldn't do better than you in my wildest dreams, which is perfect because you are the woman of my wildest dreams." Chase took a few steps forward, and a moment later I did the same. "What I'm trying to say Carlotta is that I'm sorry that my fear hurt you, that it hurt us. I'm sorry that I was too blind to see that the questions, incessant as they are, came from a place of love and well-meaning concern. I'm sorry that I've made us both miserable for the past few weeks."

I nodded. "Okay."

"There's more," he laughed and held up a hand to the crowd. "Not much more, I promise, but there is just one more thing. I love you Car. I am madly in love with you, and I know that you're the woman for me. My woman, the one I want to spend the rest of my life trying to impress, to tease a laugh from. That woman is you, and I will do whatever it takes to get a second or third chance to prove that to you."

My heart raced against my chest as his words sank in and took a firm grip of my heart. I was fully aware of the fact that all eyes in the room were on me, waiting for my reaction.

First, I smiled because Chase had done the unthinkable, he'd professed his feelings for me, in public.

He took a step forward. "Feel free to say something, sweetheart."

I laughed and took a step forward. And then another. And another.

Suddenly Chase was right there in front of me smiling at me like I was the reason he woke up each morning. "Have I told you how gorgeous you look in that dress?"

I laughed. "I believe you said breathtaking earlier."

The crowd laughed and my heart swelled at his answering smile. "By the end of the night I'll come up with something even better."

"Promises, promises," I rolled my eyes, but I could do nothing to stop the silly, little-girl-in-love smile that lit up my face. "Chase, that was really brave what you did, saying all of that in front of the busiest of Carson Creek busybodies." The crowd laughed, but I was no longer aware of them. All I saw was the man in front of me, his sparkling green eyes and his waiting smile. "I love you too Chase, but are you sure about this?"

He sighed and shook his head. "Hell no, I'm not sure about anything except for how I feel about you. Whatever it takes to make you happy, to make you love me back, is what I'll do, because the risk of getting out of my comfort zone is worth everything if you and your love is the reward."

"All I want is to be able to love you out in the open, Chase. Look around, look at how excited these people, our people are, for Pippa and Ryan. Lacey and Levi. Valona and Trey. Me and you."

The crowd whooped and hollered, whistled and clapped all around us. They were genuinely happy that another couple had fallen in love and did it here in town. "Love me anywhere you want, Car."

"Perfect," I whispered and pressed my lips to his for what felt like the first time. It was even more explosive than our other kisses, because this wasn't just lust, and it wasn't in private. This was real love, and it was out in the open in front of just about everyone who meant anything to us.

To us.

We were an *us* now.

"I love you, Carlotta, to the moon, the galaxies beyond and back."

I laughed against his mouth. "I love you too, even more than I love barbecue."

Chase laughed and pulled me in close, twirling me in a circle as the whole town cheered around us. "Care to have this dance with me, beautiful?"

"This and all the other dances to come, Mr. Mayor."

He kissed me again and the music started up, the crowd started dancing again and we were forgotten about, left in our little love bubble right there in the center of the dance floor.

It was magical.

It was perfect.

It was romantic.

It was *everything*.

And for once, it was all mine.

THE END

PREVIEW: MIDLIFE FAKE OUT

She was the one with the bottomless brown eyes that always seemed to be on the verge of tears that never fell.

Those eyes had called upon all of my protective instincts.

But that had been too much responsibility for a high school boy.

I hadn't wanted or needed that kind of responsibility.

So I'd rebelled against those instincts, and did the opposite of protecting her.

I bullied her.

PROLOGUE

Derek – *2 Months Ago*

A buzzing sound started to my left, and I flipped over to get the hell away from it. I didn't know what time it was, but the fact that I was still sleeping after the most epic awards show after-party meant it was too damn early for phone calls. But the buzzing didn't stop, and worst of all, there was a cold spot on my bed where a really hot model should have been. My eyes snapped open and I pushed off the bed, scanning the room for any trace of Sasha, or Satya, or something equally as trendy.

"Hello?"

Silence met me as the phone continued to ring. The bedroom floor no longer held a pair of tiny panties. Sheer tiny panties, if I recalled correctly, and I usually did recall, because I wasn't the kind of guy to forget what type of lingerie I tore off with my teeth. Names and jobs? Sure. To call? Almost certainly. But never lingerie. Ever.

I hurried out of the bedroom and down the hall where my black slacks sprawled across the top three steps. I distinctly remembered a long green dress with sparkles on it being somewhere near the bottom of the staircase, but now it was gone too. So were the sky high heels that capped off the longest set of legs I had ever seen. I went left at the bottom of the staircase, and the coffee table still held a half-empty bottle of champagne, two glasses beside it, one stained with a red lipstick imprint. My jacket was on the back of the sofa, along with the bowtie I'd left to hang around my bare chest, because that's what people expected of Derek Gregory, the heartbreaker of The Gregory Brothers trio. Ryan was the moody and sensitive songwriter, and Roman, as the youngest, was the goofball bad boy. We all had our roles, and I'd played mine perfectly for decades now.

I retraced my steps towards the kitchen, which was of course empty, because everyone knew models didn't eat. But there was a note. I smiled and strolled over to the counter.

"Thanks for a good time, Derek. You more than lived up to the hype. *Xoxo – Sascha.*"

I smiled even wider because she was a perfect woman. Looking for a good time with no strings and no expectations, and gone before the awkward morning after, where I would have to explain that I wasn't looking for anything serious, while a woman stared at me with tears swimming in her eyes.

"So did you Sascha, so did you."

In the big empty Nashville mansion, the only sound was my stupid phone still buzzing upstairs on my nightstand.

I took the stairs two at a time, wondering if Ryan or Roman had found themselves in the wrong type of trouble, which rarely happened, but rarely wasn't never. I quickened my steps at the thought that it could be something wrong with our father, GG, or worse, our sister Lacey, who recently decided to become an investigative journalist covering stories in chaotic regions of the world.

"Yeah, what is it?"

A familiar sigh sounded down the line, and I pinched the bridge of my nose a moment before my agent, Brody's angry voice sounded. "So you haven't been abducted by aliens or models, and you're not lying dead on the side of the road," he grumbled. "I guess I should thank the lord for tiny favors. Very tiny."

I rolled my eyes because I knew that tone. "What did I do now?" Usually I managed to balance the line between lovable bad boy and asshole perfectly, but sometimes I stepped over that line. Sometimes I jumped over it by a mile. "Well?"

"You mean other than offending our core audience

with some attempt at comedy that just came off as sexism and misogyny? Is that not enough for you, Derek?"

"You're going to have to give me more details, because all I did last night was accept a few awards, dance all night, and made Sascha moan my name until the wee hours of the morning. So tell me Brody, how have I offended our beloved fans?"

"Stop me when this starts to sound familiar yeah? *She needs to be barefoot and pregnant soon, so you can get her back in the kitchen where she belongs.*"

I froze at those very familiar words. "Yeah they're familiar. I sent that exact text to my new brother-in-law. Yesterday. Was my phone hacked? Don't worry I don't keep nudes on there," I assured him with a laugh.

"Derek," he roared over the phone. "You idiot, you beautiful, talented fucking idiot. You didn't send that to your brother in law, you sent it out to your ten million followers."

"Ten? Try twenty-three million, not that I've been counting." I tried to be active on social media, to keep the fans engaged with photos of me and my brothers, me just living my life.

"Even worse. You did hear the words I just read back do you, didn't you? Barefoot and pregnant? In the kitchen where she belongs? To our mostly female fanbase!"

"Brody it's not that big of a deal. I'll explain that it

was a private message and a joke. I'll even do a video with my sister to show them." This will blow over in a day or two, it always did.

"No you won't. I don't want you to do a goddamn thing Derek, except what I tell you to do. What I need for you to do is go away. Just for a little while. Lay low and go on a social media hiatus until I tell you otherwise."

"What? You've got to be kidding me, Brody. It was just a joke!"

"It was the wrong type of joke at the wrong time, and it offended *everyone*! Go back to that Podunk town you're from and keep a low profile, Derek. Can you do that? For the sake of your career, and if not yours, then your brothers."

"Shit, you're serious."

"Yeah Derek, I'm serious. This whole situation is serious, and I need you to take it seriously."

I worked too hard on my career to lose it now over some silly joke. "I'm listening. Go home and stay away from the spotlight." My shoulders fell in disappointment. "Anything else?"

"No," he sighed in relief. "I need to get with the public relations team and figure out how in the hell to fix this mess. Don't do anything until you hear from me. Got it?"

"Got it."

There must have been something in my tone, because when Brody spoke next, his tone had softened.

"This isn't the end of the world Derek, but it will take some finesse to handle it. Just sit tight, and for once in your life, do as you're told. Tell me you can do that."

"I can do that Brody. My career means everything to me, you know that."

"I do, but I also know you're a stubborn asshole when you want to be."

"I'll close up the house now and head to Carson Creek today," I told him, completely defeated.

"Good. And stay away from all press and social media for the next few days, will you?"

I nodded even though he couldn't see me and dropped down onto my bed. Either that or my legs gave out as the gravity of the situation settled on my shoulders.

"Yeah, okay. Sure." I ended the call and sat on my bed for what felt like forever, contemplating how in the hell I'd ended up here after such a spectacular night.

We'd won three awards last night for our last album, including Song of the Year, and today here I was.

Exiled.

CHAPTER 1
BELLA

Early mornings were my favorite time of day, always had been. The world was quiet and peaceful as the earth tilted to meet the sun's golden rays, and only a few brave souls were awake to see the first beauty of the day. It was, and had always been a private time, a time for me to gather my thoughts and prepare for the day ahead.

Now that I was officially a farmer—again—of my own free will this time, early mornings and to do lists were a necessity. For now I was a one woman operation with the help of a barely teenage boy, who was now, technically, my son.

It hurt to think about Nicola's premature death. She was my best friend, my sister in all but the biological sense, and now she was gone thanks to that unforgiving bitch known as cancer. Her death had left me and her son Everest alone in the world, forced to cope without her sunny disposition and ability to see the positive in any situation. Now it was just us, two cynics who still hadn't found a way to do more than exist without her.

That's what Carson Creek was for. It was meant to be a change, a reset for both of us, but more of a homecoming for me. I grew up here in this town and on this farm. I tilled and watered the land, fed the animals, plucked the crops and sold them all over the state. I loved farm life, it was in my blood, and I'd always dreamed of taking over the place once Ma and Pa retired. Then high school started, and the bullying, the name calling, the stares and the pointing. What fifteen year old girl didn't want to wear makeup and look pretty for hormonal teenage boys, right? Even worse than my distinct lack of desire to impress said boys, my sister would argue that I went out of my way to make sure they weren't interested, but the truth was you could only wash your hands so many times to get the dirt from under your nails. Too many hours in the barn, and not even two showers could completely shake the smell of hay. And what was so wrong with the scent of hay anyway? Without it we wouldn't have food and nourishment, but that only made me more of an outcast.

So instead of sticking around and taking over York Farm, I hightailed it out of this town as fast as I could and claimed the college scholarship that waited for me in Texas, where I'd met my best friend, Nicola.

And now she's gone.

My phone beeped and the screen lit up to remind me that quiet time was over. "Ev, breakfast is ready!" I called upstairs to the sleeping teenager, because I'd learn one month into our first nine months together that yelling was more effective than a gentle shake to wake him from his slumber. The boy slept like the dead, a skill I envied each and every day. I waited and stared at the ceiling until movement stirred above me, before I finished my coffee.

Ten minutes later Everest made his appearance. At just thirteen, he was already the same height as me. But he was at that stage where his limbs were the size of a grown man's, but he was still very much a boy, with long gangly limbs, thick shaggy black hair that looked like it hadn't seen a comb in six months, and skin as smooth and as clear as a baby's. His mother's gray eyes stared back at me, and I couldn't help but smile at the heartbreaker in training.

"You're staring again, Aunt Bella."

"Yeah, I know, and I'm not sorry at all. I was just thinking that one day soon you're going to be such a handsome stinker." He already had the makings of it, and when his growth spurt hit and his baby fat melted away, young adult women of the world would lose their minds.

Everest smirked back at me, a blush stained his cheeks. "Yeah? What am I *now*, chopped liver?"

"Nah, I wouldn't say that. Right now you're a cute stinker, emphasis on stinker. Hungry?"

"Always," he laughed and grabbed the coffee pot.

"Still too young for this," I reminded him.

Everest shrugged and poked his head into the fridge where he emerged with a bottle of orange juice. "Better?"

"Water would be better, but that is acceptable."

"Water isn't going to give me the energy I need for a long day working the fields." It was a good attempt at a guilt trip, but it wasn't good enough.

I laughed and put one hand on my hip. "Working the fields? Hardly, more like feeding some animals and cleaning some stalls, which shouldn't take more than a few hours. When you're done you can go into town and see about making some friends." We'd been in Carson Creek for a few months now, and he'd barely left the farm or made an effort to mingle with the other teens in the area.

His shoulders stiffened at my words. "I don't need to make any friends, Aunt Bella. I'm fine here on the farm. I like it here."

I nodded, because I understood the urge to hide in the face of grief. "This is your home, Ev. You will always belong here, and that won't change if you go out and make a few friends. Have a little fun."

"Not yet, Aunt B. Okay?"

I nodded. "Okay, not yet then. But soon. You don't

want to start school as the new kid."

"Fall is months away. I'll be fine."

"Okay fine. If you'd rather spend time with your super cool aunt, instead of swimming with girls at the lake or sneaking beers at the movie theater, who am I to argue?" I laughed when he rolled his eyes, enjoying this time together, because I knew that one day soon, he would wake up and view me as the enemy.

"You know if this whole farming thing doesn't work out you might have a second career as a standup comic."

"Har-har. Thanks for the vote of confidence, kiddo." I pressed a kiss to his cheek and ruffled his hair before I grabbed my phone and headed towards the back door. "I'll be fixing the fence on the south end for most of the morning, and I have my phone. Take yours with you, just in case." I called instructions over my shoulder for what felt like the hundredth time, and then I was gone, out in the already warm and sunny day.

I smiled as I hopped in my shiny blue pickup truck and headed to the fence that probably hadn't been fixed since the last York left the farm about ten years ago. It was good to be back on the farm, this time around I was older, and supposedly wiser. I didn't need to make friends or connections for my social development, I'd given up on love well before the ink dried on my second divorce, which meant I only had to do two things in this world, raise Everest into a good man, and make this farm a success again.

Both jobs were daunting, and I wasn't even sure I had it in me to do either one of them well, but those were the only things I wanted to do, which meant failure was not an option.

I had a plan. For York Farm and for Everest.

The farm was the easier task to tackle, so I focused on that while I grabbed pliers and twisted the wire around the wood posts, replacing as necessary. The land was big by family farm standards, but there was enough room to grow squash, soybeans and tomatoes on the main plots. Eggs from the chickens would sell well, because they always did, and if the trees on the west end of the property were still good, maybe apples and cider in the fall. The vertical farming buildings were already producing, so the farm could start making a profit sooner rather than later, which would help replenish the money I'd spent to fix this place up and make it livable for me and Everest.

I had a stack of parenting books in my nightstand drawer. Admittedly, that wasn't the most exciting thing to have in that particular drawer, but the books were a greater necessity than battery operated lovers. I now realized that audio books might have been better, since most of my time was spent outdoors, and that way I could multi-task, learn the best ways to parent a child who'd lost his mother, while catching up on my never-ending to-do list.

Mending the farm fence was a hell of a lot easier

than the other fence I would have to mend someday. I wasn't much of a fence-mender in the real world, more of a fence burner. Hell, even that wasn't accurate. The truth was that I was more of a barn burner, I didn't just burn the bridge, I blew up the entire structure. It was my modus operandi because life was easier to deal with that way. Scorched earth meant there was nothing to return to, or attempt to fix later.

"What a joke," I muttered as I examined my handiwork. The fence looked good, but it was the only fence likely to actually get mended. At some point in the future, before I die, I would have to reach out to my four siblings, Abel, Amara, Andora and Alex, and do something or say something. Maybe an apology or something, I didn't have a clue what would do the trick, which meant it wasn't important enough to make it onto my to-do list.

Yet.

Everest likely needed more family than just me, and I had family members in abundance. Maybe the York family could be for him what they had never been for me. Or maybe I just hadn't given them a chance.

I guess my family would go on the list sooner rather than later.

Some days being the adult, the logical and reasonable one, really sucked.

CHAPTER 2
DEREK

It hadn't taken long for boredom to set in once I got back to Carson's Creek. I lasted one week staying with Ryan and Pippa. They were disgustingly in love and I was happy for them, but I didn't need to see my brother and sister-in-law making out while trying to enjoy my morning coffee. And my niece Ryanna was as cute as they came, but she was curious as hell, and when she couldn't explore she proved to have Gregory lungs.

Roman's place was empty, so I stayed there for a few nights since I'd sold my house in Carson Creek last year. That was a good decision at the time, since I didn't spend much time in my hometown, and when I did, I had three siblings and an ornery father to stay with. But my current stay in Carson's Creek wasn't quite working out as I had hoped. After one too many eager groupies showed up at my baby brother's door, I knew my social media restriction wouldn't last long.

So I did what any reasonably wealthy and completely exiled rock star would do.

I bought a farm. Or was it a ranch? It was a giant plot of land with several smaller buildings on it that I hadn't bothered to look into as carefully as my business manager would have liked. It was out on the outskirts of town, which made it perfect in terms of privacy, and there was enough room that I could probably turn one of the buildings into a studio. This exile might be the perfect time to start building my credentials as a producer, at least that's what I told myself, but seven weeks in, and I hadn't even called a contractor. Or hired anyone to tend to the overgrowth which was out of this world.

I thought about asking my neighbors next door, since the rumor in town was that someone had actually purchased or rented the York Farm, but I hadn't seen any evidence of their existence beyond a shiny truck and crops growing day by day. *Great, they were actual farmers,* which probably meant early to bed and early to rise.

The neighborly thing, the southern thing to do, would be to go over there and introduce myself. Maybe offer some muscle once in a while and hope they would do the same for me.

Another time, maybe. I needed, no, I wanted to get the studio built as soon as possible. It would give me something to do, and it would keep me out of trouble until Brody reached out to say I could make trouble again, and do it publicly. I got up and dumped my lukewarm coffee down the sink, I then went about my daily ritual of discreetly checking the internet to see if the women of the world still hated me, and—yep—they did. Instead of stewing over it and cursing the world for my bad luck, I headed outside, determined to scope out the perfect studio space.

The building closest to the main house would be ideal for convenience, but I could put in a small unpaved path if one of the other buildings proved better suited. It was so quiet that I could hear mosquitoes whizzing by my ears, birds chirping in the distance, even the crunch of overgrown foliage under my boots.

It was too quiet.

But I heard a vehicle in the distance, close enough that it was either a visitor for me, or someone at the York Farm was out and about.

My phone beeped with a message from Roman. *"Where the hell are you?"*

"I'm at home. Grounded."

That's exactly what it felt like. I was back to being fourteen and forced to sit in my room and do nothing, not one damn thing, because I'd gotten caught doing something stupid. *Some things don't change*, I thought and smiled to myself.

"We're here," was the next message that came through.

I made my way back to the front of the main house, an act that took even longer than walking the property of my Nashville mansion. Both of my brothers stood on the front porch looking around at the property, probably wondering what in the hell I was thinking.

"Hey, what are you guys doing here?" Not that I wasn't happy to see them, but I hadn't had any visitors in weeks. "Didn't even know you were in town," I told Roman.

Ryan shrugged and ran a hand through his long blond hair with a sheepish smile. "Pippa thought you might be going nuts out here by yourself and made me come."

"Gee, thanks man." I snorted and punched his shoulder.

"I would've come out if you had asked, but you're not exactly the begging type." He wasn't wrong. I didn't need a group to amuse myself, at least that's what I told myself, but I had been going a little stir-crazy out here on my own.

Roman shrugged and clapped me on the back with a playful smile as he gestured to the land before us. "I just wanted to lay eyes on the old hovel, see what kind of dumbass trouble you got yourself into now."

"It's hardly a hovel," I told him and shoved my elbow into his side. "The place just needs some tender loving care, which I plan to give it. With the help of a landscaper and a contractor." Even as I said the words, a vision of what the place would look like came to me.

"A contractor?" Ryan's arched brows nearly disappeared into his hairline. "For what exactly?"

I nodded for them to follow me around to the back of the house. "Afraid I'm going to open up a place to rival Dark Horse?"

"Hell no," he growled. "Nina is happy where she is, so anyone you could get would be a poor imitation."

I rolled my eyes. Nina was a damn fine chef and woman, but I had no desire to run a restaurant. "I'm going to turn one of the buildings into a studio, produce more tracks, maybe some albums for other artists. What do you think?" My brothers and I were close, very close, but we weren't the touchy feely sort to talk about our feelings until our voices went hoarse.

Ryan grinned. "Yeah? That's a good idea. Plus, the main house is big enough if you want to put the artists up yourself."

I hadn't thought about that, but it wasn't a bad idea. "Like those old artist communes back in the day," I mused, suddenly liking the idea more and more.

Roman snorted. "Of course you would decide to do this after my first album is done and on the shelves. But it's a good idea, a good way to keep busy until your current shit storm blows over."

"Don't remind me," I grunted. "One little mistake

and I'm being tarred and feathered." I still couldn't believe it, and I was pissed off. But I promised Brody I would be smart and that I would listen. "Anyway..." I said in search of a change of topic and coming up empty.

"Meet the new neighbors yet?" Ryan asked with a smirk.

"Nope. I guess they're real farmers or something." I did think it was strange that I hadn't even caught a glimpse of them yet. "Or vampires, possibly ghosts."

Ryan rolled his eyes. "Pippa was right, you are going crazy."

"Maybe the ghost farmers are just good at hiding from the misogynistic rock star," Roman mused and pointed to a figure off in the distance.

I followed the direction of his finger and let out a small gasp, because it was an actual person. "Unbelievable." I guess I had started to believe the place might be empty. Carson Creek specialized in gossip, but they didn't always get it right.

"Let's go introduce ourselves," Roman said and started towards the fence before anyone else had agreed. Typical youngest kid, always did whatever the hell he wanted.

"I guess we're going to meet the neighbors," Ryan said with a knowing smile that normally would have set me on edge, but nothing in my life was normal right now and it was all because of social media.

No, it was my fault. Plain and simple.

By the time we got to the fence Roman had already introduced himself, though it probably wasn't necessary because the kid already knew him.

"Oh wow. I love The Gregory Brothers, but your new album is incredible. Been listening to it on a loop since it came out," the teenager with black floppy hair had an awestruck grin.

Roman stood a little taller at the compliment. "I would offer a signed CD, but I wouldn't even know where in the hell, um heck, to get a CD anymore. But I'll definitely get something to you."

The kid laughed and shrugged. "You don't have to do that."

"You kidding? Without fans I wouldn't be shit, I mean hell," he sighed and scrubbed a hand over his face. "You know what I mean right kid?"

"Yeah," he nodded. "I do. The name is Everest, by the way." He finally noticed me and then Ryan with wide gray eyes. "Holy shit, do you guys live next door?"

"I do," I told him and stepped forward with a handshake. "I'm Derek, and I just bought the place. Haven't seen anyone next door at all."

Everest nodded and glanced at the property with a critical eye. "What are you planning to do with the land?"

"My first plan is to get the land cleaned up so I can see what my options are, but I'm going to turn one of the buildings into a recording studio."

"Cool," he nodded and looked around. "I can help clear the land if you want."

"Yeah?" I didn't know, given the current state of things, if that was such a good idea. "Why?"

He shrugged. "My aunt keeps talking about going into town and making friends. If I have something else to do, especially a job, she might lay off awhile longer."

I frowned. "You don't want to make friends?" What kind of teenager didn't want friends, especially a good looking kid like him that could easily be very popular?

"I just got here, and things have been rough. My mom passed away, and I'm just taking it easy for a while." He scanned the grounds once again and turned to me with those gray eyes that looked as if they'd seen too much. "I spotted some peach trees on the south end of your property, if you're interested in tending them, they look to be bearing fruit." The way the kid breezed over the dead mom information called to me, I'd done the same when we lost our mother.

I smiled at his mature way of speaking. "You grew up on a farm?"

"Nah, but my aunt did, and she knows all kinds of stuff."

"So why aren't you helping her?" Roman shoved his hands in his pockets and leveled Everest with a look.

"She only lets me feed the animals and clean their living areas because she wants to make sure she can handle the workload when I become the most popular kid in town." He snorted his opinion at that aspiration. "Anyway, you know where I'll be if you decide you want some help. It's a big job."

We all smirked at how easy the kid was with us. "Everest, why did you guys choose Carson Creek?" There were bigger towns and bigger farms throughout the state.

He shrugged at first, and then lifted his eyes to the blue sky and blinding sun. "She grew up here. Said she didn't much like it here back then, but that it was a great place for us both to start over, so here we are. Oh and this is her family's farm."

No. it couldn't be. The universe couldn't be so cruel to me, not now when I was exiled to my hometown. The universe would not trap me beside my biggest regret, would it?

There were five York kids, and three of them were girls. It could just as easily be Andora or Amara, but my gut knew that it wasn't. It was the svelte York sister, the one with the bottomless brown eyes that always seemed to be on the verge of tears that never fell. Those eyes had called upon all of my protective instincts. But that had been too much responsibility for a high school boy. I hadn't wanted or needed that kind of responsibility. So I'd rebelled against those instincts, and did the opposite of protecting her.

I had bullied her. Badly.

"One of the York girls," Ryan mused. "Which one?"

"Bella York," a rich feminine voice answered as she

came to a stop beside Everest. She was as beautiful as ever. Gorgeous with her long limbs, strong and lean. Her white tank top showed off her shoulders and toned arms, a pink bra peeked from behind one of the straps. But her legs were the real superstars, encased in denim that looked damn near painted on. A floppy hat sat on top of her thick brown hair that hung halfway down her back, or would have if the wind hadn't picked it up and swirled it around her body. She put a hand on Everest's shoulder and smiled. "The Gregory Brothers. Hey Ryan. Roman." She didn't say my name or even look in my direction, and I wasn't at all surprised.

"Bella York," Roman purred and leaned in with an appreciative smile. "You always were a pretty thing, but holy hell woman. I'm of legal age now," he reminded her and wiggled his eyebrows.

Bella laughed, and the sound was thick and rich. "Thanks Roman. And congratulations on your solo and group success. You guys are all over the place."

"We took a risk, and it paid off." Ryan shrugged like it was no big deal. "What are you planning to grow?"

"Quite a bit actually. Soybeans will be our biggest crop, there will also be squash and tomatoes, and hopefully some apples from the orchard. I also have a vertical farm with plenty of herbs and leafy greens. A lot of stuff," she said with an embarrassed laugh. "Sorry."

"Don't be," Ryan assured her. "I own Dark Horse, it's

a high end restaurant in town, and my chef Nina loves to come out and pick fresh food. She would love this."

I watched as she chatted easily with my brothers, and wondered to myself how it was possible that she had gotten even prettier over the years. She was still willowy with this innately delicate look about her, but now there was also a strength about her, inside and out. "It was great to see you guys, a real blast from the past. But I need to get back to it," she said and thumbed in the direction over her shoulder. "Tell your chef to come by anytime to check the place out. I'm happy to show her around." She took a few steps back, brown eyes smiling wide at my brothers before she turned to Everest with an affectionate smile.

"What about me?" I shouldn't have said anything. I should have just left it well enough alone. She didn't like me, probably hated me, and she had good reason to ignore me completely. But that just wasn't my style.

Annabella York froze and turned slowly to level me with an icy glare. "What about you?"

I took a step forward and licked my lips. "Am I welcome anytime?"

She flashed a sexy smile, and I swore my knees gave out a little. She was hot as hell fully clothed, and I couldn't help but imagine what she would look like in nothing at all.

"You, Derek Gregory are welcome, never. Not ever, even if there's an end of the world disaster. Unless of course you have a fondness for the taste and feel of shotgun slugs."

"Ouch," Roman groaned and then laughed.

With a pointed look at me to make sure I got the hint, she turned and walked away, long legs eating up the space quickly.

My brothers roared with laughter at her insult, looking at me with questions in their eyes that I refused to answer. "I can't wait to hear that story," Ryan said around a loud guffaw.

Even Everest laughed. "Wow. I'm pretty sure Aunt Bella hates you, and she likes everyone. *Everyone*," he emphasized. "Sorry," he added with a shrug. "It was nice to meet you guys. All of you." He waved and walked off, shaking his head with an amused smile.

As soon as Everest was out of earshot, Roman laughed even more loudly. "What the hell was that about man?"

"Ancient history," I growled and walked away from the fence, putting as much distance between me and Bella York as possible. With her so close, her hatred so palpable, it didn't feel all that ancient. It just felt like another thing that I would have to apologize for.

Eventually.

Some day.

Later.

Bella & Derek's story continues in Midlife Fake Out.

Also by Piper Sullivan

Midlife Fake Out: Bella & Derek

Midlife Love Story: Carlotta & Chase

Midlife Love Affair: Lacy & Levi

Midlife Valentine: Valona & Trey

Midlife Do Over: Pippa & Ryan

Healing Love

Dueling Drs, Book 6: Zola & Drew

Rockstar Baby Daddy, Book 5: Susie & Gavin

Unfriending the Dr, Book 4: Persy & Ryan

Kissing the Dr, Book 3: Megan & Casey

Loving the Nurse, Book 2: Gus & Antonio

Falling for the Dr, Book 1: Teddy & Cal

Curvy Girl Dating Agency

Forever Curves, Book 8: Brenna & Grant

Small Town Curves, Book 7: Shannon & Miles

Curvy Valentine Match, Book 6: Mara & Xander

Misbehaving Curves, Book 5: Joss & Ben

Curves for the Single Dad, Book 4: Tara & Chris

His Curvy Best Friend, Book 3: Sophie & Stone

Curvy Girl's Secret, Book 2: Olive & Liam

His Curvy Enemy, Book 1: Eva & Oliver

Small Town Protectors (Tulip Series)

That Hot Night, Book 12: Janey & Rafe

To Catch A Player, Book 11: Reece & Jackson

Cold Hearted Love, Book 10: Ginger & Tyson

Hero Boss, Book 9: Stevie & Scott

Dr's Orders, Book 8: Maxine & Derek

Mastering Her Curves, Book 7: Mikki & Nate

Kissing My Best Friend, Book 6: Bo & Jase

Undesired, Book 5: Hope & Will

Wanting Ms Wrong, Book 4: Audrey & Walker

Loving My Enemy, Book 3: Elka & Antonio

Bad Boy Benefits, Book 2: Penny & Ry

Hero In My Bed, Book 1: Nina & Preston

Accidental Hookups

Accidentally Hitched, Book 1: Viviana & Nash

Accidentally Wed, Book 2: Maddie & Zeke

Accidentally Bound, Book 3: Trish & Mason

Accidentally Wifed, Book 4: Magenta & Davis

Boardroom Games

His Takeover: An Enemies to Lovers Romance (Boardroom Games Book 1)

Sinful Takeover: An Enemies to Lovers Romance (Boardroom Games Book 2)

Naughty Takeover: An Enemies to Lovers Romance (Boardroom Games 3)

Boxsets & Collections

Small Town Misters: A Small Town Protectors Boxset

Misters of Pleasure: A Small Town Protectors Boxset

Misters of Love: A Small Town Romance Boxset

Misters of Passion: A Small Town Romance Boxset

Kiss Me, Love Me: An Alpha Male Romance Boxset

Accidentally On Purpose: A Marriage Mistake Boxset

Daddies & Nannies: A Contemporary Romance Boxset

Cowboys & Bosses: A Contemporary Romance Boxset

About the Author

Piper Sullivan is an old school romantic who enjoys reading romantic stories as much as she enjoys writing them.

She spends her time day-dreaming of dashing heroes and the feisty women they love.

Visit Piper's website www.pipersullivan.com

Join Piper's Newsletter for quirky commentary, new romance releases, freebies and contests.

Check her out on BookBub

Stalk her on Facebook

Printed in Dunstable, United Kingdom